MW00948434

PRAI

NORM & GINGER ENTER THE HIDDEN

"*Norm and Ginger Enter the Hidden* is a magical, mysterious adventure that will leave young readers clamoring for the next book in this exciting new fantasy series."

—SUSAN DIAMOND RILEY, award-winning author of *The Sea Island's Secret* and *The Sea Turtle's Curse*

"Any novel that has a 'Seeing Eyeball Crystal Ball Sandwich Cookie' as part of the story is too much to resist. And author Betty Fudge makes the reader glad to take in book one of this delightful series. Her protagonist, Becky, is pulled into adventures that take her from New York to Scotland, Ireland to Vermont, and places in between in *Norm and Ginger Enter the Hidden*. There are witches and dragons and shapeshifters. There are magical animals, including a turtle, praying mantis, dragonfly, and a basset hound for good measure. Fudge's smooth, polished writing pulls the reader along and into a fantastic world of good and bad with subplots to enjoy. I hope book two comes swiftly."

—JOHN CARENEN, prize-winning author of the Thomas O'Shea mystery/thriller series and *Keeping to Himself*

"You won't want to put this fantasy book down until you are finished. A strange day at school is the beginning of an unfolding web of mysteries, with lots of twists and turns that keep you turning the pages. A young girl, a puppy, and four beautiful, mysterious stones help to drive this adventure. You'll love this story!"

—KIMBERLY GALE CAMPBELL, author of nationally regarded cookbooks *PlantPure Nation Cookbook* and *PlantPure Kitchen,* and head of culinary development and education at PlantPure, Inc.

"Betty Fudge has created a new magical journey that will impassion the next generation of readers. A journey that rivals some of the greatest books of our time. Masterfully written for those ready to take on a new and exciting adventure."

—PAUL VILLATICO, MED, head of school (retired)

"Fantasy readers ages 8–12 who look for stories about friendship, alliances, and adversity will find the first book in the series, *Norm & Ginger Enter the Hidden*, an adventure that grabs hold from the very first line . . . The epic story that evolves is filled with action and excitement, with a dose of wry humor sprinkled in for good measure . . . *Norm & Ginger Enter the Hidden* is a vivid fantasy about friendships, alliances, mysteries, and problem-solving that will intrigue and delight children looking for mystery and adventure. It's a captivating leisure read that leaves the door open for more."

—MIDWEST BOOK REVIEW, Diane Donovan, senior reviewer

"In these strange times, Betty Fudge brings us the story of pure fairy-tale whimsy that we all need right now. Amidst a gang of enchanted critters, Irish fae, and even dragons, one loveable floppy-eared basset hound embarks on a journey to rescue her human from an evil spell. Mysteries abound, as not everything is as it seems and not everyone can be trusted. Book two can't come quickly enough!"

—DANIELLE KOEHLER, author of *The Other Forest*

Norm and Ginger Enter the Hidden

by Betty Fudge

© Copyright 2021 Betty Fudge

ISBN 978-1-64663-399-9

All rights reserved. No part of this publication may be reproduced, stored in a retrieval system, or transmitted in any form or by any means—electronic, mechanical, photocopy, recording, or any other—except for brief quotations in printed reviews, without the prior written permission of the author.

This is a work of fiction. All the characters in this book are fictitious, and any resemblance to actual persons, living or dead, is purely coincidental. The names, incidents, dialogue, and opinions expressed are products of the author's imagination and are not to be construed as real.

Published by

3705 Shore Drive
Virginia Beach, VA 23455
800-435-4811
www.koehlerbooks.com

NORM & GINGER
ENTER THE HIDDEN

BOOK ONE

BETTY FUDGE

VIRGINIA BEACH
CAPE CHARLES

To Kaitlyn and Jordan
Norm and Ginger will always belong to you

CHAPTER 1

*Someday you will be old enough to
start reading fairy tales again.*

—C.S. LEWIS

When things go wrong, they go way wrong. That didn't mean sixth-grader Becky Miller had to like it, but she did have to live with it. Later—and there'd be a lot of later, because that was how her life was about to reshape itself—she'd be able to think about all the things that had gone wrong. That wouldn't make the result any better, wouldn't even make it understandable. It would only clarify the picture. And her place in it.

Point One. She wasn't early getting to school. She wasn't exactly late; she made it with seventeen seconds to spare. But Becky liked to be early. She liked to be in her seat well before the first bell. And on this day she wasn't. Nothing she could do about that; she was late because her mother was late, but Mrs. Reynolds didn't accept people's mothers as a reason for lateness. Becky didn't know why her mother was late. She seemed distracted, as though something was wrong, and when Becky thought about it, she knew her father had been distracted, too. But that happened sometimes. They hadn't explained to Becky what was troubling them. Adults could sometimes be very odd, and Becky hadn't asked. She would wish, later, that she had.

Point Two. She'd taken her science report from the printer and placed it on the kitchen table. Which is where it still was. She'd put it there so as not to forget it—and forget it was exactly what she had done in the frenzy of getting her mother organized enough to get out of the house. Mrs. Howard taught science, and Mrs. Howard was no more receptive to excuses than Mrs. Reynolds. This would cost Becky ten points. At least.

When they finally reached the school gates, Becky unclipped her seat belt, kissed her mother on the cheek, opened the car door and, as she leapt to the ground, shouted "Byemomthanksloveyouseeyouthisafternoon!" and legged it across the school yard, out of breath and puffing like one of those old-time steam locomotives with cow catchers on the front you sometimes saw on TV movies. The ones with leather-skinned old men in boots and ten-gallon hats, and fresh-faced young women in gingham dresses carrying parasols. She wasn't the only one still making her way in to school, but she was the only one running. Because not everyone liked to be in their seat well before the first bell. Not everyone cared if Mrs. Reynolds, or whoever the teacher, was cross with them. And not everyone had a best friend like Jessica.

Becky and Jessica had known each other forever. Their fathers worked together. Their families socialized together. Neither of them had a brother or a sister, but that didn't matter because they had each other, and their parents—and Mrs. Reynolds—often said they were like twin sisters. Not identical twins, because *identical* is something they weren't, but that didn't change the fact that when one of them thought something, the other was often thinking exactly the same thing. Or that Becky or Jessica would start a sentence and the other would finish it. Or that they liked the same parks, the same burgers and pizzas, the same sodas and the same colors.

Jessica was a strawberry blonde with a creamy white complexion that refused to tan. The best friends had spent countless hours together this summer baking in the sun and swimming at the community swimming pool. Becky's skin turned a beautiful golden brown while Jessica's turned lobster red, peeled, and then exploded with freckles. Thousands of freckles. A Milky Way of freckles.

As usual, Jessica would already be at her desk, which was, of course, right next to Becky's, and Becky had missed the chance for a catch-up before class began.

Becky burst through the door and slowed. Fighting to catch her breath, she steadied herself. Walked more slowly across the floor. Seventeen seconds. That's how far she was from a nightmare that one day soon she would fear she'd never wake up from.

There was her desk. She looked at Jessica, and she knew something was wrong. Becky had never seen that look on Jessica's face before. She wished she wasn't seeing it now, because it wasn't pleasant. At all. Why would her very best friend stare at her like that?

She reached back for her bookbag so that she could sling it onto her desk. Then, just one more step, she'd be in her seat, Jessica would be next to her, the bell would ring, and all would once more be well.

But it wasn't. A leg was suddenly in front of her, sticking out to trip her. It was Jessica's pale leg. Impossible, but it was true.

Becky tried to avoid the face plant, leaning back, arms waving, hoping to get her balance, as well as her dignity. It only bought her a second, but it was long enough to get another look as Jessica's skinny, freckled leg darted back under the desk.

Becky's left cheek slammed into the floor followed by the right wrist she had extended as she tried to stop her fall. She felt something warm around her mouth followed by a stinging pain on her elbow. There was a buzzing sound in her ears that she realized was laughter. She struggled to her knees as the teacher quickly made her way down the aisle, impatiently hushing the class.

Mrs. Reynolds was one year away from retirement. She had seen everything in her decades of teaching, and she knew how to control her students. She had a zero-tolerance policy for what she called "Tom

Foolery," and her stern warning was enough. The laughter stopped.

Blood trickled from the small gash on Becky's cheek. It pooled around the edge of her mouth before dripping down her chin and onto the floor. Mrs. Reynolds helped her stand, then gently handed her a small white towel as she gave her a motherly pat on the arm.

"This will make your cut feel better. I will walk you to the office and we can call your parents. Sit down and I will pack your book bag. Everyone, open your books and turn to page ninety-seven." She waved her arms at the students, motioning for them to turn around and get to work, but this time they disregarded her instruction. All eyes remained glued on Becky while Mrs. Reynolds collected the books and papers littering the floor.

Becky couldn't bear to look at her classmates, so she stared at her knees. Her eyes stung with hot tears that she quickly blinked away. She was not going to cry. Not here. Not in front of everyone. She wanted to get out of there. What was taking so long? She heard a blowing sound from across the aisle. It was Jessica, calling for her to look her way. With her head still tilted downward, she cautiously moved her eyes in the direction of the sound.

Jessica glared at her with a smug smile. Her posture was stiff. She sat with her hands folded, elbows braced on the desk, as she leaned forward in a catlike pose, ready to pounce on its prey.

"Why did you do that? Why did you deliberately trip me?" Becky tried to stay calm, but her voice trembled in disbelief and anger. This made no sense. Any other classmate, and especially that horrid boy Kenneth, and she might have believed it. But not Jessica. And yet that smug smile remained. In fact, it had grown larger and more exaggerated as Jessica's eyes darted toward the teacher, eagerly awaiting her opportunity.

When Mrs. Reynolds stepped away to collect the pencil that had rolled farthest across the floor, Jessica leaned across the aisle and beckoned. Becky leaned forward, hoping for an explanation. She didn't get one. In fact, what Jessica whispered made no sense at all.

"You will leave. She is coming for you and you will go with her. Olwen is coming. Through the mirror."

Becky's mind whirred with questions. *The mirror? What mirror? WHO was coming for Becky? This Olwen person? Well, who was Olwen? And why did Becky have to go?* None of this made sense, especially the way Jessica delivered her message. Flat. Emotionless. It was as though someone—something?—had taken control of Jessica. Because that tone was not Jessica. Not the Jessica Becky loved like a sister. Not at all.

And what about the eyes? Becky's heart was beating so loudly she felt sure the whole room must hear it. Where were Jessica's eyes, those beautiful sea blue eyes so often crinkled in laughter? All Becky could see in their place was black, expressionless emptiness. Was something heating this room? Because sweat was running down Becky's shirt. Her gaze moved to the other students. Every one of them was staring at her. Every one of them had black, menacing eyes. The walls were closing in. She had to get out of here. She had to get out of here NOW.

Mrs. Reynolds crawled from beneath a desk, securely clutching the pencils that had fallen from Becky's bookbag. The gray hair that was always neatly tucked into a French bun now hung carelessly over her forehead, but Mrs. Reynolds seemed not to notice. Through the gray strands Becky could see two black disks where Mrs. Reynolds's eyes should have been. Becky struggled to control her breathing. This was not Mrs. Reynolds, because it couldn't be, and that was not Jessica, because that could not be, either. So who?

A dream. Of course! She took a deep breath, speaking slowly to herself. *Calm down, Becky. You're in a dream. Wake up and everything will be fine.*

But it wasn't. She dug a fingernail into her leg, expecting the jolt that would wake her and bring her back to the classroom, back to today, back to her friend, her teacher and the classmates she knew. And it didn't happen. She struggled to stand and felt blood from her cut knees ooze towards her ankles. This was no dream. Her best friend was possessed, her teacher was possessed, the whole class was possessed, and all that mattered was to get out of here before whatever had taken possession of them entered her, too. Adrenaline carried her to the door, but Mrs. Reynolds was already there, gliding effortlessly to block her escape. The teacher leaned forward, placing her face close to Becky's ear. When Becky tried to back away, Mrs. Reynolds wrapped an arm around her shoulder and pulled her close. Her expression was calm, her smile reassuring and gentle. Everything was just like every other day—except for the eyes. Eyes that were black disks in which irises swirled red like molten lava.

"Becky. Sometimes we don't look for trouble, but trouble comes looking for us, and trouble has found you, my dear." She continued in a friendly tone that nobody but Becky could hear. "It's afterwards that everything is understood. Remember this when you go to the FALLA-HACHET." The last word gurgled out of her mouth, sounding like someone was holding her head under the water.

What did she say? Where am I going? What is a "fallen hatchet" and what does it mean? I have got to get out of here. NOW.

But then, as fast as the chaos had started, it ended. Mrs. Reynolds tucked her hair neatly back into her bun, fixed Becky with a look of affection from eyes that were the same color as they always were. She took the bookbag in one hand and Becky by the other, escorting her in friendly silence to the front office, delivering her to the school nurse. Just before going back to her classroom, she said, "See you tomorrow morning, Becky. Tell your mom I said hello. I hope your leg feels better soon."

And then she was gone, and Becky sat in numb silence as the nurse put antiseptic on her cuts, chatting cheerful nonsense that Becky blocked out because her mind was on other things. What was she going to tell her parents? How could she make them believe what had happened? Did she believe it?

When her mother arrived, Becky saw an expression she hadn't seen before. There were dark circles under her eyes, and they weren't caused by sleep deprivation. Mascara smudges coated the outer corners of her eyes. This wasn't just shock at the sight of Becky's scraped knee. Something else was wrong. Seriously wrong.

Once outside the school, her mother walked way too quickly to the closest park bench and motioned for Becky to sit beside her.

"First, how do those scrapes feel? Are you okay? I'm sorry all this is happening on the same day." Her usually composed tone was rushed.

"ALL this?" Becky felt her voice tremble, but she tried to remain calm.

"We did not see it coming but your father was—" Her voice trailed off as she paused to clear her throat. "He was let go from the university this morning."

"Fired? Why? Why would they do that? He's one of their top professors. He's assistant department chair. They can't do that!"

"There are some things we will need to talk about, sweetheart, but it can wait."

Any time her mother inserted "sweetheart" into a sentence, Becky knew there was bad news. From her mother's expression, Becky knew it was something very bad. There was no need to press her mother for details because she knew it would go nowhere. Now what should she do? She couldn't tell her parents that her teacher, her classmates, her VERY BEST FRIEND, were possessed. If you wanted a definition of something that really sucks, this was it.

Becky had learned the direct approach isn't always the most productive. You can ask your parents all kinds of questions, and if they don't want to answer, they won't. They might make you think you are getting the answer—Becky's parents were very good at that—but, in reality, you're getting fluff. And she would know it. But there are other ways of finding out what you want to know.

At home, Becky went quietly to her room, saying that she had homework to do, and sat just as quietly on her bed with her door open. Her parents were downstairs speaking to each other in soft tones, but Becky could hear snippets of their conversation. She didn't get the whole story because her mom and dad didn't need to repeat what they both already knew, but she did find out that her father's sacking had something to do with his work.

Becky's father was a cultural anthropologist. Becky knew anthropologists study how people behave. Not individual people; that was a job for psychologists and Becky knew that her father didn't think much of psychologists. No, anthropologists studied whole groups of human behavior. And the groups of people her father was interested in were called *cultures*.

Becky had been getting a bit bored when her father's explanation had gotten to this point, but he had gone on talking and she had listened because that's what she'd been brought up to do—

to listen to her parents.

"And that's culture," her father had said. "In some cultures, no one listens to children. In some, they do. If you ever hear someone say, 'Children should be seen and not heard,' that's their culture speaking. And there are other cultures where no one listens to old people, or to their own parents. Those are different cultures."

She'd had to stop herself yawning, but then it got just a little bit more interesting when he said that he was particularly interested in medieval and pagan cultures, and that meant something to Becky because that semester her class project was about what life had been like in Europe in the Middle Ages.

So, something in his work had got him fired. She wondered if it was something he'd found out that other people didn't want anyone to know about. Becky's father and Jessica's father carried out research together at the university. Becky wondered if her father's firing and the strange events at school were connected somehow.

It seemed clear from what she was hearing that Jessica's father had not been fired. Maybe Jessica had learned from her dad some details of Becky's father's firing. She thought about calling Jessica and asking her, but every time she was about to dial, a small but insistent voice coming from she didn't know where said very firmly, *DON'T!*

Becky didn't get much sleep that night. She tossed and turned, worrying about what tomorrow would bring at school. She thought about pretending to be sick, just to give things another day to calm down, but in the end she knew she had to go back. At least this time she would be more prepared. She made sure her mother dropped her off early the next morning, wanting to get into class before Jessica, but when she got there, Jessica was already seated.

Nonchalance, that was the word. *Behave as though you don't have anything to worry about.*

"Hi Jessica. Did you watch 'Riverdale' last night?"

They always chatted after every episode, so this seemed like a safe way to start the conversation. But not this time. Jessica turned up her nose as though she had smelled the thing she liked least of all in the world, which happened to be sushi. Just to make sure that her message was understood, she turned her back on Becky and started talking to another girl. The two girls whispered, then started laughing.

Feeling her cheeks flush, she dared another pass. "Jessica, I don't know what I did to make you mad, but I'm really sorry if—"

"Your dad is ridiculous. Thankfully, my mom said he wasn't able to drag my father down with him with his crazy theories." Her tone was harsh and her teeth clenched.

"You're my best friend. What theories? I am in the dark here. Tell me, what theories? What did your mom say? My parents haven't told me anything. You said Olwen is coming. Who is Olwen?"

"Olwen? Don't say that name. My mother was *sooo* right about your parents, and *you!*" Jessica turned her back, raising her hand to get Mrs. Reynolds' attention. "Please can I switch seats with someone else? Becky is bothering me."

From there, and for days to come, things went downhill. On the good days Becky was subjected to strange looks, whispers and muffled laughter from Jessica and the new group of girls that she hung out with. The bad days involved direct, in-her-face name-calling and insults, usually about her father, who The Jessica Tribe called "weirdo," "fairy-whisperer" or "gnome man." Her parents had protected her, or so they thought, from the details of her father's firing, and of his research, but that only made matters worse because Becky could only assume her father had done something scandalous. Why was she taking so much abuse? What in his research could have been so horrible? She had to put a stop to this.

Becky needed to find answers so she could mount a defense against these horrible things they were saying about her dad. But Internet searches turned up few clues. There was no mention of a scandal, and when Becky searched the university's website for references of her father's past research, or classes he taught, everything had been removed. She knew there had been scientific write-ups about his work because her mother had shown them to her in the past. From the look of their website, it was as if her father had never worked there. *What now?* She needed to get the information from the source—her parents. This was going to require finesse. *What if I let them know how The Jessica Tribe is treating me? That will ruffle Mom's feathers. Surely that would make them want to tell me something, maybe not everything, but more than I know now.*

Becky decided to bring it up at the dinner table when both parents would be together. *I will just leave out all the details about that insane morning with my possessed classmates and Mrs. Reynolds.* Becky raced downstairs feeling confident in her plan. Why hadn't she thought of this before?

Once seated at the table, she noticed that her parents were unusually quiet. Her mother pushed her mashed potatoes around on her plate without a word, and her father sat glued to something he was reading on his laptop. They might be distracted, but she was in no mood to wait.

"I don't understand why Jessica is being so mean to me. Ever since you left your job, she and the other girls have been saying terrible things. They are calling you fairy whisperer and gnome man. Dad, why would they call you that?" She stopped there. Hopefully, that was enough to get them to spill the beans.

"Try to ignore them. Jessica is being ridiculous and very rude. I would not want a friend like that," her mother offered with a lame smile before taking a bite of her cold potatoes.

"I agree," her father said. "Find a new group of girls. We could look at another school in Manhattan. How would that sound? Just start with a fresh slate at a new school."

Horrible idea, Becky thought. She wished she hadn't said anything to her parents. Instead of uncovering something useful, her parents were making the ridiculous suggestion to change her school. Unfortunately, things were about to get even worse.

She arrived home on that Friday afternoon to be greeted by the sight of men from a moving company packing up her family's belongings. She looked from one parent to the other, her eyebrows raised, waiting. Her mother announced, with every sign of cheerfulness as though this was perfectly normal family behavior, that they had decided to move to rural Vermont. A farmhouse, her mother said, had been in the family for more than a century, which was news to Becky. Not only had they never visited it, but the farmhouse had also never even been mentioned. And now they were going to live there. Becky, a girl accustomed to the surroundings of a city that never slept, was going to have to make a new life with nothing around her but trees, fields, bugs and rivers. *How can they do this to me?* But they didn't seem to see any problem.

CHAPTER 2

It takes time to build castles.

—IRISH PROVERB

Three thousand miles away, in County Antrim, Northern Ireland, a woman named Catriona strolled through the herb garden that grew, mostly wild, along the edge of her property overlooking the sea. She loved the intoxicating smell of rosemary that grew abundantly in the fertile soil. The temperatures had been warm, and her garden was bursting with mint, lavender, thyme and basil, as well as blueberries and more flowers than she could identify.

She gazed out at the sea and inhaled deeply. She loved this place, and today the ocean was especially beautiful as it rippled against the rocky shoreline. Barely a breeze stirred, and the calm ocean sprawled out before her like a glass landscape that was the perfect shade of blue.

And into this happy scene Catriona watched as something threatening intruded. What looked like a large bird glided toward her, its wings barely flapping. Catriona's eyes narrowed. For this was no ordinary bird, and the warning it carried alarmed Catriona before her words had even been spoken.

"Marin," she whispered. "It's been a long time. Do you bring news of my sister?"

The bird landed on the limbs of a young willow, inches from where Catriona was sitting. It hopped to the ground and walked to the back door, waiting for Catriona to open it. What followed when it was safe inside the house would have frightened most people, but she had seen it before. The bird stretched its wings. And then the wings became slender arms, and feathers became skin—gray at first, but turning to snowy white. Catriona gazed with a wonder that would never fail her, no matter how often she saw this happen. The bird had become a girl, three feet tall, her eyes sparkling with silvery white brightness. Those hypnotic eyes were always the first things Catriona focused on each time she saw the creature. Long hair flowed down the girl's back in ringlet curls streaked with blue green, like the sea. Small gossamer wings laced with a thin blanket of downy black feathers fluttered gently on her back. This was Marin.

"I bring news of the house. The house in Vermont. It is empty no longer."

Fear touched Catriona's heart. They had chosen the house in Vermont to keep secret what should never be known. She had hoped that all of it could be contained, safely hidden. But now—

"Who has moved in there?"

"Professor Miller. Is he your cousin? Your nephew? No matter. He is there with his wife and their daughter, Rebecca."

"Why have they chosen to live in Vermont? I suppose he can travel to New York from there?"

"He has no need. He is a professor no longer. He was removed from his job."

"Do we know why?"

"He was studying customs from the past. He offended forces much stronger than him. He left in disgrace."

Catriona weighed what she had just been told. "Well, it is what it is. I imagine an American professor, especially one with our lineage, discovered that there were such forces in the world. But what has he discovered? And . . . the dollhouse?"

Marin nodded. "The dollhouse."

"It is well hidden?"

"I do not believe that any adult would find it. But an eleven-year-old girl . . . with all her curiosity? And time to search?"

Catriona sighed. "I had hoped so, after all this time. And those forces you speak of. They will have an interest in helping her find it. It would set the powers of darkness free."

"And put her," said Marin, "in great danger."

"Does my sister know?"

"I cannot say what Fiona knows. Nor do I know what she might do if she became aware."

"Watch her, please. If she leaves her castle in Scotland, you must tell me immediately. I don't believe she has ever found the diary, because if she ever laid a hand on my necklace I would know, and the diary and the necklace are together. I have often thought of paying her a visit so that I can retrieve them and keep them forever out of her hands. But she would not make me welcome. And if I searched and failed to find them, she would know that there was something to be found. She knows the stories, because we learned them together as young girls. But I can only think that she doesn't believe them. Whereas you and I . . . we know them to be true. And we know just how much trouble would follow if those forces were unleashed once more onto the world."

"I, too, am sure the diary is there, because I cannot enter the castle, and it can only be the diary's magic that keeps me away. But if she leaves, I will know, and you will see me again."

Catriona removed from her desk an old leather book that she gripped as if holding a powerful weapon. She said, "Let us not despair. I am aware of another who will be sent to help at the appropriate time."

"Who will be sent? You have never spoken of it."

"My diary speaks of a guardian who will be sent to—" Catriona's voice trembled. "Never mind. I would like for you to find someone to keep watch for the arrival of the guardian. Someone who could help us."

"Where will the guardian appear?"

"Most certainly Vermont. A protector for Rebecca and perhaps an intermediary. Something to interpret the creatures that will be on her side, but forces that she cannot understand. And something to make her stay away from those others who would do her so much harm."

Shortly after Catriona and Marin's meeting, another winged creature descended on a stream in Vermont. The creature spotted a praying mantis on a tree limb and landed next to it. Fearful that it would be eaten, the insect froze on the branch, its limbs arranged so that it looked like nothing more than a twig. The winged creature spoke.

"It's no good trying to hide, Rothschild. I can see you."

"Please don't hurt me," the mantis said.

"I have no intention of hurting you. And I wouldn't dream of eating you, which is what you're really afraid of. I have instructions for you. Things are going to be happening around here, threatening things, and if they're not dealt with in exactly the right way, the results will be ruinous. But I am here to help. Now listen while I tell you what you must do."

CHAPTER 3

"Do not wait to strike until the iron is hot;
but make it hot by striking."

—WILLIAM BUTLER YEATS

s it turned out, Vermont was not the social death that Becky had feared. In fact, five months after being moved there, she liked it. The early morning din of Manhattan streets, which she had thought to be the most comforting sound in the world, had been replaced by a low hum from the steam radiator that warmed her room. Outside the only sound came from the wind whistling against the old wooden window frames of her bedroom, and on evenings when the weather was warm enough, the chirps of frogs and crickets. During the day, the yard would spring to life with more birds than the girl had ever seen.

Becky awoke to silence. There were no birds chirping at the moment, because it was still dark. It was Saturday, and no need to get up, no rush to be somewhere. *Why am I awake?* she wondered. Something had awoken her, but what? There was a noise.

Perhaps it had been a dream, but if it was, and she had now woken from it, getting back to sleep should have been easy. As sleep refused to come, she listened and heard nothing. Sweeping her hand across her forehead to clear the tousled long auburn hair that blanketed her eyes, she discovered with surprise that she was soaked with sweat. She looked up towards the dark ceiling and wondered what to do. Early though it was, she was wide awake.

She scrambled out of bed and looked for her slippers. She was certain she had left them right there when she got into bed last night. *So where are they? Am I mistaken? Could they be in the closet? The bathroom?* Becky was not accustomed to bouts of forgetfulness.

She got down on her knees and began to feel under the bed. No slippers. *But what is this?* Skimming the old plank floors with her fingers, she discovered a loose section of boards. *Why would anyone loosen the floorboards here?* She crawled under the bed and dug her index finger into the side of the nearest loose board. It tilted slightly, revealing a new surprise. From the crack between the tilted board and the others spilled a bright blue light that lit up the whole room with pulsing turquoise shimmers. Eagerly, she pulled the floorboard from its resting place to see where the light was coming from. And she found a box.

Without hesitation, she reached into the hole, lifted the box and placed it on the floor beside her bed. It was warm, and it rattled in her hands like a lidded pot of boiling water. She nudged the lid carefully to one side, afraid to remove it entirely. A strong current of hot air blasted her face, blowing her hair upwards. Her eyes closed against the onslaught, her cheeks grew hot and felt chapped. She leaned back and caught her breath as the rush of air subsided.

Inside, she found four large stones. The mysterious shimmering light was coming from the blue stone. Nestled beside it she saw three more stones. A large red stone the size of a golf ball, a green stone in the shape of a figure eight, and a small square black stone. She picked up the glowing blue stone and held it in her hand. It was warm—almost hot. As she held it, the light shifted toward the window, pointing toward something outside as though transmitting a signal. *But to whom? To what?*

Becky scrambled to her feet and went to the window to pull back the curtain. The stone responded by emitting a stream of light downward, in the direction of the chicken house in the yard. She strained to get a better view. The sun had not risen, but a faint touch of pink offered enough visibility to reveal a path seared through the grass. That path had not been there when she went to bed the night before. It disappeared over the crest of the hill, but she could see smoke rising off the grass from the newly blazed trail. The stone vibrated in her hands, disrupting her focus, making her almost drop her prize. She touched her windburned cheeks as she considered the possibility that she might be dreaming. She allowed Mrs. Reynolds's prophetic warning to ease back into her mind, then dared to speak it.

"'Sometimes we don't look for trouble, but trouble comes looking for us.' I think this might be the trouble you were warning me about," she said aloud to herself.

Her voice trailed off as she concentrated on the stone. Grasping it tightly, she raced toward the kitchen, tripping over her forgotten slippers. She groped for the side of the bed with her free hand just before her knees crashed to the floor. Catching her breath, she stopped long enough to slide her feet into the furry slippers and stuff the stone into her pajama pocket as she made her way outside.

The October morning was dawning with a bone-chilling cold, jarring Becky as she raced out of the warm kitchen onto the icy porch. She hopped back into the mud room to dig through the jackets that hung on the hook by the garage, settling on a warm parka that belonged to her mother. *This will do.* She shoved her hands in the pocket and found a bonus. Work gloves! "Jackpot," she whispered.

She tucked the glowing blue stone into the jacket pocket, noticing that it had become almost too hot to handle with her bare hands. Its light had grown more intense, sending out bursts of blue and silver pulses, pointing in the direction of the chicken house. She could feel excitement growing. Something was out there—perhaps danger—but nothing was going to stop her from going outside to find out.

She made her way down the smoldering path just as the sun hinted its arrival. Shivering violently, she faced the direction of the sunrise, but there was no warmth. Instead, an icy breeze sent pain across her chapped cheeks. She took a few more steps forward, wrapping her collar tightly around her neck as she fought against a wind that was trying to force her backwards. She knew it wasn't possible, but the wind seemed almost personal, as if it was sent to obstruct only her. Her long auburn hair was pulled back into a loose ponytail, so the icy chill crept easily down her neck toward her back.

Something had been waiting outdoors. In the shadows at first, but now hovering close, an icy winged creature blasted her. Thunder pounded in Becky's ears as the creature exhaled another snowy blast of air. She gasped to catch her breath. Her legs felt weak, and her thoughts raced as panic built.

"How could I freeze to death just a few yards from my own house?" she mumbled.

The stone responded, becoming so hot that it warmed her entire body, even through the thick layers of her jacket. Energized by the warmth, she continued down the path, slowing only momentarily to take the stone carefully from her pocket. No sooner was it freed from her jacket than it lifted out of her hand, hovering a few feet from her face. It cast a vibrant glow that illuminated the shadows, allowing Becky the glimpse of something moving. The winged creature had retreated but remained close, and though Becky strained to get a better look at it, she could make out only shadows and outlines of gray. Her gaze shifted as the stone traveled toward the chicken house and rested in mid-air, spinning above the entrance. Bright blue and turquoise shimmers sprayed in all directions followed by crackling and popping sparkles. The air grew hot, sending anything that resembled winter, or ice, or cold, into retreat. The last blue and silver sparks rained down to illuminate her destination.

Blue light spilled from inside the chicken house, and a warm spring breeze blew across Becky's face. Frantic clucks from the chickens suggested that something was disturbing them. Her instinct was turn and run, yet she felt emboldened. As she reached out to open the door, she heard something completely out of place. She hesitated. She gasped, then laughed as she stepped inside.

"It can't be. No way!"

But it was. In the corner, half hidden, sat a puppy. Thick brown and white fur peeked from behind mounds of fresh straw, its beautiful brown eyes were smiling at her. As if it knew her, the puppy's tail wagged enthusiastically, sending straw flying. Becky stooped to the ground, hoping it would come to her. The puppy loped clumsily from the nest, tripping momentarily on its long ears that nearly touched the ground. After a short skid, the puppy ran into her arms. This was the happiest moment Becky had felt in as long as she could remember. As the chickens gathered around, nervously checking out this new addition to the flock, the puppy licked Becky happily and curled into her lap.

Around the puppy's neck was a thin black collar. The blue stone sat on top, generating light and heat. Becky ran her hands around the collar, feeling for the clasp and, as she released it to inspect the collar, the blue light dimmed. Instantly, cold air invaded, sending a shiver down her back. She frowned, then reattached the clasp, and light returned to the stone. This was as strange as strange could be, but Becky was wrapped up in her new friend. She scooped her up and wrapped her inside her coat before hurrying back to the house and tiptoeing up to her room.

Together, they sat by the opening in the bedroom floor. Becky looked in the box; the three remaining stones were still inside.

What now? Should she tell her parents everything that had happened? They wouldn't believe her. How could they? If she told herself this story, she wouldn't believe it, either. She lay the box aside, cuddled the puppy and whispered, "They have secrets, so this can be *our* secret."

She reached for the collar and opened the clasp. As before, the blue stone went dark. The black leather collar felt soft and appeared old and worn. In large lettering, the word *SINSEAR* was lettered in fancy script.

"*Sinsear*. What is that? Your name?" The puppy enthusiastically wagged her tail, as if recognizing her name. "That sure is a strange name!" She went to her computer to type in the word. Sure enough, the word was there. "This word is ancient Irish. A Gaelic word meaning Ginger. I like it. Your new name will be Ginger."

But if her parents saw the collar, they might have questions she couldn't answer. The solution was easy. Becky placed the collar carefully inside the box with the other stones and tucked it back into its hiding place. But now arose another mystery, because when she leaned down to put the box back into its hiding place under the floorboard she saw another, larger box. *Had it been there before?* She hadn't seen it, but big boxes don't just appear. It must have been there all the time, for it was dusty and cobwebbed, like something that had been undisturbed for a very long time. A sudden tiredness came over her. She had had enough excitement for one morning. The new box could wait. She put the boards back in place and pressed them down firmly. She'd look at the new box when she was ready.

As she pressed the boards into place, a puff of what must have been dust wafted into the air, making her sneeze. Something tiny flew, undetected, to the ceiling and landed there. Ginger wiggled close to Becky, turning circles, wedging securely into her lap. Looking into her puppy's beautiful brown eyes she whispered, "This will be our secret. You have a new home now, and a new family."

CHAPTER 4

Honey is sweet, but don't lick it off a briar.

—IRISH PROVERB

Becky had told Ginger that she had a new home, but it wasn't quite as simple as that. If Ginger was going to live here, her parents would have to agree. But would they? This was going to need careful handling. Becky decided to wait until her parents came down for breakfast and surprise them. There was a simple formula to this process—one part adorable puppy and one part equally adorable daughter. Becky knew she wasn't always adorable; in fact, she knew she could be downright difficult. But she could switch to adorable at will, especially when she had a good reason. Add to that an adorable puppy and a dash of parental guilt for moving them from Manhattan to the middle of nowhere, and Ginger has a new home.

Becky watched the clock. Any minute now her parents would be awake. She rehearsed her story, but what about a backup plan if they asked lots of questions? Did she have a diversion strategy? Too late, they were awake.

Ginger was the first to hear them when they entered the hallway. Whether by instinct or from some other cause, she knew what role she was playing, and she bolted to greet them as they made their way down the narrow staircase. Her tail swished in large sweeping motions, happily thumping the walls. Her tongue dangled carelessly from the side of her mouth. With each step, her tongue lopped out further from her jowls.

"Well," said her mother. "What do we have here?" She plopped down on the first available step, halfway down the staircase. Ginger scrambled to greet her, but her ears got tangled up in her paws and threatened to send her tumbling to the bottom. Becky's mom leaned over and lifted Ginger the rest of the way, pulling her safely into her lap.

Her father stepped around the chaos and walked casually toward Becky, smiling. This small positive signal sent a welcome wave of relief. She needed this to go smoothly. It had been an interesting morning, to say the least. After a warm greeting with her mother, Ginger spread the love by dashing over to snuggle up with Becky's father.

"What a cute puppy you are." He bent down to give Ginger a hug, then turned back to Becky, waiting for her to speak.

Ginger had greased the wheels. The ball was now in Becky's court. She cleared her throat and tried to sound casual.

"I heard her crying in the backyard early this morning. I let her inside. She seemed so cold. I think someone just dumped her somewhere and she found her way here. I've named her Ginger. Doesn't she look like a Ginger?" Realizing that she was beginning to blabber, she reeled herself in and cut to the bottom line. "Can we keep her?" She flashed her best innocent grin and placed her hands carefully into a prayer position. "Please? I'll take care of her, and we really need a dog now that we live in the country."

Her parents looked at each other with that parent telepathy thing that they liked to do. Becky was always amazed at their ability to make big decisions by just staring into each other's eyes. Today their ability was excruciating. This was too important. She wanted this puppy. She *had* to have her. The silence continued as Becky stared back at them, trying to read their expressions. If Mom spoke first it was a done deal. If Dad spoke first there was more negotiating to be done. There would be a bigger inquiry. Her story could unravel. Just the thought of that was making her sweat. If they saw her getting sweaty that would trigger concern and more questions. She shifted her legs nervously. *Don't get fidgety,* she thought. *Stay calm. It's just a puppy. Never mind that there are laser beam jewels and who knows what else buried in the floor. Maybe the puppy is a product of some bizarre magical spell.* Her stomach felt a little queasy.

She felt sweat drip down her back. Sensing that serious negotiations were underway, Ginger made her plea audible with a gentle *woof* that broke the silence. Becky's mother looked down at Ginger who had planted her rump squarely on her right foot and was leaning firmly against her leg. This time Ginger's tongue was inside her mouth and she gave them a loving gaze before flopping to the floor.

Her mother spoke first. "I think she is an adorable puppy. I like her a lot. If it is okay with your father, I am good with it."

Becky knew what that meant. She was home free! With little or no resistance, both parents gave the green light to keep Ginger. The only caveats: they needed to make sure her owner was not looking for her; they must take her to the vet; and she would be Becky's responsibility. Check, check, double check. It was decided. Ginger could join the Miller family.

As happy as Becky was to have Ginger, the first week back at school was very stressful. Becky felt certain that Ginger had canine superpowers that would erupt in front of her parents, so for the first three mornings she whispered in Ginger's ear the same command. "Today you are a normal dog. Don't do anything to draw attention. No light show. No special powers. Please. Just be a normal dog."

Then she would be forced to endure the torture. She would try to pay attention in class, but also be on guard, expecting a call to the office. A frantic call telling her that something had happened. Something bad. Then everyone at school would start talking about it. Whispering behind her back. Just as they had done in Manhattan when Jessica had stopped being her best friend and became hateful. The first three days were difficult.

By Thursday morning when nothing unusual happened, Becky started to relax and settle into her routine. In third period math the phone rang on the teacher's desk. It was the office. Becky felt her heart skip a beat. She watched as the teacher frowned slightly and looked in her direction. Sweat started dripping down her back.

"Becky, you are needed in the office. Better take your bookbag in case you don't make it back to class. Make sure you get the homework assignment." Her teacher sounded serious.

Becky could feel the stares. Everyone was looking at her as the class fell silent. It was starting all over again. Something had happened, and one of her parents was here to get her. Maybe even the police. Everyone would be talking about it tomorrow. She did not want to get up out of her seat. *Not more name calling, please.* "Gnome man" would be replaced with "laser dog girl." Or worse.

"Becky. Did you hear me? You are needed in the office. Your mother is here."

Becky heard a few giggles. She packed up her bookbag without a word, feeling the sensation of the room as it started to spin. *Is this what a panic attack feels like?* She made her way down the deserted hallways to the office. Thank goodness everyone was in class. Maybe she could keep this quiet. Tell everyone a dentist appointment had slipped her mind. But, as she arrived at the office, she saw her mother standing in the entrance with two secretaries close to her. *Well, great.* That was the end of any hope of privacy.

Her mother had a big smile. All three women were laughing. "Sorry to interrupt class, sweetie, but you forgot your permission slip for tomorrow's field trip to the planetarium. Today is the deadline to get it turned in."

The relief was so great, she almost sank to the floor. This was a sign that everything was going to be fine. She took the permission slip and raced back to math class. She strolled back into the class, beaming. She smiled as she waved the document in the air. "Forgot my permission slip," she said.

The next week, they took Ginger for her vet appointment and were told that Ginger was a purebred basset hound, in excellent condition for a puppy that had been abandoned, and approximately one year old. It came as no surprise to Becky that Ginger's owner never stepped forward to claim her. Her fears that Ginger would erupt with superpowers in front of her parents faded. Whatever a superpower character might be, Ginger seemed the opposite. She had no athletic abilities of any kind. Far from leaping tall buildings in a single bound, she could hardly jump off the sofa without doing a faceplant. She was uncoordinated. She tripped over her own ears. When she wagged her tail, it threw her off balance and if she didn't happen to be standing on a flat surface, she would roll downhill.

After several weeks of watching Ginger struggle, Becky considered retrieving the collar from its hiding place. Maybe if she let Ginger wear it, just for an hour, it might help her puppy overcome some of the challenges. But what if it restored whatever magical powers Becky had thought she might have? And how would she answer questions from her parents about where it had come from? All in all, it was better to leave the collar where it was.

One thing Becky knew, and that was that having Ginger made the transition to Vermont and a new school much easier. Every day after school she looked forward to coming home and telling Ginger about her day. She felt that Ginger understood every word, and that was super power enough for Becky.

CHAPTER 5

It's no use carrying an umbrella if your shoes are leaking..

—IRISH PROVERB

By the time spring arrived, Ginger had learned the rules of the house. It was as though she had been there her entire life. As the days grew warmer, she and Becky spent most days outside at their favorite spot by a creek that ran through the edge of the farm. Becky loved spending time there, and although Ginger was not much of an explorer, she never let Becky go alone. Ginger would sit and watch as Becky looked under creek rocks or searched for small frogs or turtles. Ginger would rest her nose in the flowing water, blow bubbles and scan the surface with her soft brown eyes as the occasional leaf floated by. While most dogs have a much better sense of smell than humans, Ginger's was far worse. If she had to rely on scent to find someone, or heaven help, to get home after becoming lost, it would be bad news. For that reason, she never strayed away from home, always keeping the house or at least the chimney in sight. Her sense of direction was also dismal, adding to her tendency to stay close. But however bad her senses of smell and direction might be, Ginger's hearing was amazing. If anyone opened a cookie wrapper or took a bite from a potato chip anywhere in the house, Ginger heard it and came running. She hoped to get a morsel, and usually she did.

Ginger considered herself a house dog, and a member of the family. Not quite human but not a yard animal either. She liked it cool in the summer and warm by the fire on cool Vermont nights.

For her part, Becky occasionally thought about the items hidden under the floor in her room. She considered opening the box and putting the strange collar on Ginger to see what might happen. Every time it crossed her mind, she reconsidered. Things were going too well. After everything that had happened the year before, she wanted calm. She needed calm. That collar was not calm.

It was early on a Saturday morning and Ginger was asleep in her favorite spot next to the kitchen radiator. A popping sound woke her, and she quickly rolled onto her feet, waiting for the next sound. The house was quiet, and Ginger remembered that everyone had gone outside. She was inside, alone. She heard the faint scratching coming from inside the pantry. *A mouse,* she thought.

As she plodded toward the pantry, she heard it again and she quickened her pace. The pantry door was open, and she entered without fear. As a huntress she would be useless, but she could certainly intimidate a mouse.

The pantry appeared empty except for the usual canned goods and paper products. She waited, her ears perked in anticipation. The next sound was a large thud that caught her off guard and sent her retreating back to the radiator. Another thud. She approached slowly, sniffing the ground even though she knew it was pointless. As she peered into the pantry, she identified the problem. One of the boards on the back wall of the pantry was displaced. The board hung loosely, dangling by a long nail. She felt relief, and with renewed confidence trotted over to inspect.

Behind the gaping hole made from the loose board she saw a large object, partially visible. She walked closer. Her nose touched the loose board. Carefully, she nudged it and it hung in place, appearing to latch open. With the opening now large enough she stuck her head inside.

Behind the pantry wall was a hidden space, large enough to be considered a room. Next to the opening were several packages that looked like gift-wrapped presents. She approached the packages slowly, sniffing the floor and then stopping to listen. Her long droopy ears perked up when she heard the faint scratching sound again, coming from the largest box. She backed up a few steps. The scratching sound stopped, so she edged closer, curiosity taking over as she leaned forward perking her ears as close to the packages as she dared. Without warning, the smallest box shifted and tumbled forward landing on her front paw. Her bravery evaporated, and she wailed a loud growl-bark, skidding backwards, taking the oriental rug with her as she retreated out into the living room. She sat hard on the bunched-up rug that was jammed against the sofa, panting and relieved that nothing had followed her to safety. Regaining her composure, she returned to the kitchen to assess the damage. The explanation was obvious. She had bumped the packages with her paws and the small box had rolled off the pile. That must be it.

She walked part of the way back into the hidden room. As she entered, her body blocked the light from the kitchen, preventing her from seeing inside. An unexpected cold draft blew across her nose and then sucked her inside. She felt her feet dragging across the wood floor. Her rear toenails caught on the threshold giving her a momentary foothold against the hidden force. Even through her panic, her senses remained focused. Something was in the room. With her. She struggled, digging her paws into the old pine floors. She heard a flapping sound coming toward her, but in the darkness she could not see it. It was close now. She could feel its cold breath pressing down on her.

A sharp pain shot through her front paw; her toenail had broken off as she clawed the floor. Ignoring the pain, she intensified her struggle. She thought about Becky and was even more determined to break free. She had to warn her family. She went on the offense, biting and clawing at the force dragging her into the room.

As suddenly as the attack started, it ended. Ginger felt the icy grip release her, and she sprawled backwards, rolling violently into the kitchen. Dazed, she felt her legs bang against the doggie door that led to the outside, and she scrambled to her feet to make her escape. Fueled by adrenaline, she rushed blindly, barking, tail tucked, and ears blown back, not daring a backward glance. She saw the alarmed looks as she approached her family. *Good,* she thought. *Follow me. Inside. Now. We must leave this place. You cannot live here another minute.*

She ran back toward the house, pausing to look in confirmation that they were following her. Thankfully everyone came inside. She led them to the pantry, panting anxiously as she watched Becky's father step inside to investigate. Now they would see the danger. Now they would leave this house—and take Ginger with them.

Rather than screams of terror, Ginger heard happy sounds coming from the room. She watched as they rushed to find flashlights. Becky's parents disappeared into the hidden room and quickly emerged toting gift-wrapped packages. Her mother dusted them off as her father removed the label from the largest box and read it.

"This package was supposed to be sent to someone in Aberdeenshire in Scotland, but so much of it is faded I cannot make out anything else. We have family in Scotland."

When Becky heard this, she lit up. "I never heard you talk about family in Scotland."

"The wrap looks very old," her mother said. "There's no telling how long this has been tucked away in there." She reached for the closest kitchen cloth and draped it over the top of the largest box, plowing away a heap of dust and grime to reveal the tarnished silvery wrapping paper. Her father moved behind the box and pushed it through the hidden room's threshold and into the light of the kitchen as her mother moved with lightning speed to remove the other smaller boxes from their hiding place, almost as if she had discovered buried treasure.

Her mother grabbed a flashlight and stepped back inside the hidden room. "Becky, do not follow me. Please stay in the kitchen and clean up these packages and unwrap them. It will be fun to discover what is inside them. I will help your father see what is inside this hidden room." Her voice trailed off as she disappeared into the darkness, leaving Becky and Ginger with the mysterious artifacts.

Ginger growled at the boxes and tugged gently at Becky's sleeve. This was a bad idea. But no one paid her any attention. She watched as Becky opened the largest box, positioning her face next to Becky's hands as she pulled away the wrapping paper to reveal the contents hidden inside.

The largest box stood five feet tall and at least as long. Once Becky was able to tear and pull the musty cardboard away from the structure, she revealed an antique dollhouse. It was much like the farmhouse they were living in, a white two-story Victorian house with a wraparound porch and gabled windows upstairs. The bottom story was adorned with two large stained-glass bay windows. The only difference between the dollhouse and the Millers' farmhouse was a sprawling turret at the back, an imposing feature with dark shingles and a small attic window. Latches on each side allowed Becky to open the house and reveal the interior room layout. Ginger sniffed the upstairs room, which was a miniature version of Becky's bedroom.

The other boxes contained an assortment of furniture, rugs, household accessories, and dollhouse people. When Becky unpacked the toy dog, the fur on Ginger's back bristled and she wrinkled her nose with her most menacing version of a snarl. Becky stared at the collection of items, silently considering their significance, but she hadn't completely lost sight of Ginger's reactions.

"You don't like this dollhouse at all, do you?"

Ginger wagged her tail enthusiastically and growled at the dollhouse. Becky returned to the kitchen to find her parents still inside the hidden room. She listened, momentarily, to their whispered voices, trying to get the gist of the conversation before making herself known. The fragment of conversation made Becky recoil as she heard her father say, "With everything I know about our family, this room may be the link we were looking for. I want to set up my research lab here. I think it is our best shot to underst—" His voice trailed off as the creaking sound of the old wood floor where Becky was perched betrayed her. Her parents stopped talking and stared at her, smiling.

"Sorry to interrupt," Becky fumbled. "I opened the boxes. There is a cool dollhouse in there and it looks almost identical to *this* house. Dad, it is so big, would you help me take it up to my room?"

"I will be right there to give you a hand." He cheerfully responded without sticking his head into the kitchen to continue the discussion.

"That's wonderful, Becky. I'll come up later and check it out." Her mother sounded distracted.

Becky hesitated for another moment, searching for signs of stress from her parents and waiting for them to explain what she had overheard, but no explanation was offered. There was something she wasn't being told. Her parents were good at surprises, and sometimes when Becky knew she wasn't being told something, she felt a shiver of excitement because she sensed that what they were keeping secret was something she was going to enjoy. But this wasn't like that.

Ten trips later, Becky and her father had relocated the dollhouse in her room and placed all the accessories in the corner for further inspection. She watched as Ginger nervously paced around the room, tail uncharacteristically tucked between her legs. Becky frowned, remembering the night she'd discovered the objects hidden in the floor. *What's the chance this dollhouse was part of the mystery?* she wondered.

After several minutes of pacing, Ginger reluctantly joined Becky when she saw her pick up the first piece of furniture and place it inside the house—a teal blue sofa in the downstairs sitting room. Becky closed one eye and braced for something to happen. But nothing did. *Well, that's a good sign.* Just a normal dollhouse with normal doll furniture. What had she been worrying about? She patted Ginger on the head, letting out a huge breath.

She continued furnishing the dollhouse, placing all the rugs, furniture and people inside. The last thing she put in the house was the cute dog.

"Look, it even comes with a miniature Ginger. Let's put her in my bedroom. I'll put her on my bed where you like to sleep. Too bad the people are just statues. They don't bend or I would have the little girl sitting on the bed, too. That's it. Now everything seems to be inside."

When nothing had happened during the placement of the furniture Becky felt strangely disappointed. "Well, I was expecting some fireworks. But not even a tiny spark. What about you Ginger, did you expect something exciting to happen?"

Ginger wagged her tail slowly but kept her eyes on the house.

Becky's mother entered the room. "Wow, that dollhouse is beautiful! You did a great job decorating it. Your father and I found another box in the secret room. It wasn't wrapped like the other boxes, and I almost stepped on it."

She handed Becky the box. "Looks like some additional items for the dollhouse. Come down to eat. Dinner is ready."

"I'll be right down. Thanks, Mom."

Becky examined the wooden box before gently turning it upside down. It appeared to be old, with ornate scrollwork on top and sides. It had a lock, but no key, but that didn't matter because it wasn't locked. When she opened it, a pleasing smell of lavender flowers filled the room. Inside were several items for the dollhouse. An antique rocking chair, a writing desk, and a full-length wardrobe mirror. It was much larger than the other pieces of furniture. And there was something else. Becky gasped, picking up the mirror for a closer look.

The top of the mirror was lined with four colored stones—one red, a blue stone, a green figure-eight stone and a black stone in the shape of a square. Becky felt a shiver creep down her spine as she held the mirror in her hand. Something was going on, some connection between the boxes under the floor, the dollhouse and this mirror. She wanted to think it was something good, but all her senses told her it wasn't.

The sound of her mother's voice interrupted her thoughts. "Your dinner is getting cold. Please come downstairs!" Her mother was always polite, but there was an uncharacteristic shrillness in her voice. Becky stumbled to her feet. In her haste, she felt the mirror slip from her hand, and only just managed to grab it before it hit the floor.

Another shout, this time from her father. "Becky! Do you hear your mother? Come down to eat."

She placed the mirror on the floor and dashed downstairs without a backward glance. Ginger listened to the sound of Becky's feet thumping down the stairs. She trotted to the bedroom door and peered down the empty hallway, listening for the sound of her family gathered at the dinner table. Ginger liked to sit under the table during meals because everyone sneaked nibbles to her, especially Becky's dad. But tonight, she had something more important to do. She didn't understand how she knew, but that mirror belonged inside the dollhouse. She felt a need to put it in there.

Ginger picked up the mirror, gently resting it in her mouth, as she made her way toward the dollhouse. A sweet pungent taste filled her mouth reminding her of the time she took a bite of the muscadine grapes that grow along the fence line of their farm. Ginger did not like grapes and the unpleasant surprise caused her to gag and she placed the mirror back on the floor. In the mirror's reflective surface flowing water appeared. What was worse, it was leaking onto the carpet. This was bad. Would this flowing water turn into a torrent? She stepped away from the mirror and the image disappeared. Ginger took the opportunity to complete her task. She winced as she picked the mirror up in her teeth and made her way to the back of the dollhouse. As she leaned over to put the mirror inside, something pulled it from her mouth and dragged it into the back corner of the upstairs bedroom. She flopped down, inches away from the porch, and stared into the windows of the house, waiting to see what would happen. Ginger knew something would happen. She could feel it.

CHAPTER 6

Say little and say it well.

—IRISH PROVERB

Before Becky got to the bottom of the stairs, she had made the decision to ask her parents some questions. They had been acting strange. Something had happened back in New York, and she was determined to find out what it was.

When she got to the kitchen her parents were waiting, and the food was on the table.

"Sorry I didn't hear you, I guess I was concentrating on the dollhouse. Dinner smells great."

"I need to call Aunt Fiona and ask what she knows about the dollhouse." Her father's voice was casual, the way he might mention a neighbor they see every day.

"And the secret room," said Becky's mother.

Becky had never heard them talk about any aunt in Scotland. "I didn't know we had relatives in Scotland. Who is Aunt Fiona?"

"We also have Aunt Catriona in Ireland, on your father's side, of course."

Now Becky knew she was being kept in the dark. Her mother's cheerful voice when mentioning this second aunt that no one had ever spoken about before inflamed Becky's curiosity. She held her mouth open, spinning her fork in circles in the air, her eyebrows raised to signal she wanted details "More. I want more. Who are these people?" She'd known that look since she'd been no more than a preschooler. She thought of it as *the glance*. It meant there was something they did not wish to discuss in her presence. And there it was. The flicker of their eyes. The knowing, secret communication. Was it to protect her? Or exclude her?

Becky knew her father wasn't going to disclose much. "I only met Aunt Fiona one time, when I was much younger," he said. "I was with my parents and we visited her, in Scotland. It was that visit and meeting her that sparked my interest in world history. It's why I became a history buff. We should take you there sometime. To visit her."

"What did you see there that made you want to become a history professor?"

"I would have to take you there so you would better understand. We'll visit someday."

Her mother joined in. "Your father has decided to renovate the hidden room, make it into his lab . . . I mean his *study*." She laughed as she reached for the mashed potatoes.

"What are your plans, Dad? Are you going to continue to teach somewhere?" It was the first time Becky had asked. Maybe she had been afraid to know.

"This is a great new opportunity for me. For all of us, as a family. I've been so bound up in writing historical publications, I haven't been doing enough of the active research I've always loved. So that's what I'm going to do. The research will be archaeological as much as historical. We are excited about it. Especially because your mother will be able to work with me."

Before Becky was born, her mother had worked as a molecular

biologist. Becky also knew that, however much her mother loved her and wanted to be the one who looked after her instead of hiring a nanny, there would come a time when her mother would return to her work as a scientist.

Despite her father's disclosure, there was a vagueness in his answer. A casual but determined refusal to state facts. Becky loved her parents as much as they loved her, but that didn't mean she couldn't feel irritated when they didn't tell her things she thought she had a right to know.

"Will the two of you need to travel?" she pressed.

"Oh, no, we will be doing our work from here. We will fill you in as we know more."

Yes, thought Becky. *I just bet you will. You're not filling me in now.* And then her mother changed the subject, confirming Becky's suspicion.

"What do you think of that dollhouse? It will be interesting to hear what Fiona has to say about it. It's obviously very old. I bet it's valuable. You're lucky to have it. I'm sure Fiona can tell us more. And I'm anxious to hear more about the reason for the hidden room."

Her father turned to Becky. "That reminds me: don't go in there. You could get injured. I plan to run some temporary lighting. And Keep Ginger away from there as well, okay?"

"Sure, no problem. It looks creepy in there. I don't think Ginger likes it. I am surprised you think it would make a good office."

"Yes, I think it has potential. In fact, I am headed there now to start my work." He stood. "I cooked dinner, so I leave it to you guys to clean up here. But first, what time would it be in Scotland? They're five hours ahead of us, aren't they? So, this still could be a good time to call Fiona. I'll do it from upstairs."

On the other side of the Atlantic, things were happening that would, in the end, tell Becky far more about the dollhouse and what it meant than anything her parents were about to say. Something that would bring Becky knowledge, but also great danger.

Catriona had asked Marin to go as close as she dared to what she called "the castle" in Scotland, and to let Catriona know if it looked as though her sister Fiona was about to leave her home. What neither of them knew was that Fiona did, indeed, intend to leave the castle—*forever*—because the stately manor had simply become too big to manage by herself.

And so Fiona had asked her personal assistant, Abigail, to arrange to sell the estate that had been in the family for centuries. Fiona planned to retire to somewhere smaller, but still in the same small area of Scotland. But that was about to change with the phone call from distant Vermont.

At first, Fiona was delighted by the call from her nephew, and asked Jeff questions about his daughter, Becky, and how things were going for them at the family farmhouse. She said she had decided to sell her Scottish estate and how sorry she was that Becky would not be able to visit it while it was still in the family. But when the conversation turned to the discovery of the hidden room and especially the dollhouse, Fiona's tone changed.

"Is the dollhouse still in the box? It really should not be played with."

"But why, Aunt Fiona? It's in Becky's room. She's very responsible. She won't break anything."

"I'm not concerned about that. It's just . . . oh, dear. I wish you'd called me as soon as you found that room. I don't want to get into this over the phone, but has Becky mentioned anything about the dollhouse?"

"Like what? What's wrong with it?"

"*Nothing* is wrong with it. Nothing inside that house would harm Becky. But there are stories. Old stories that have been told in the family for generations."

"I've never heard them. What stories?"

"Oh, probably nothing. But . . . oh dear, I wish you'd left that dollhouse where it was. Look, I'm coming to see you. I'll look at the room and the dollhouse. For now, tell Becky to leave *everything* where it is. Jeff, please don't move the dollhouse again. Do you promise? Leave it where it is. I'll call as soon as I can to tell you my travel plans."

Fiona went into the kitchen to brew a cup of chamomile tea in hopes it would help her sleep. She had spent most of the day cleaning out the attic and boxing up the last of the antique Christmas ornaments that were too fragile to trust to movers. Even though her back was sore and she felt tired, she could not fall asleep. Not after that phone call. She sat and waited for the kettle to boil and thought of all the pots of tea she had brewed in this kitchen. The house was quiet, but she could hear the gentle popping of the radiators that warmed the drafty Scottish manor house that she had called home for over fifty years. The house had been built in the 1500s and renovated many times by family members lucky enough to live here on the forty beautiful acres of rolling hills with a river that flowed through the edge of the property. It had seen so much, most of it good, but some things were best not thought about. And there was, of course, *the story* handed down through the generations and no doubt exaggerated and distorted.

Fiona was not a person to meet trouble halfway. She hoped *those days* were over. She even hoped that one day, she and Catriona, the sister who was so much like her and yet so different, might reconcile. Perhaps, when she had moved into her new home, she might pick up the phone and make the first move. It could be so much easier if they met somewhere other than here.

The kettle's whistle pulled her attention from nostalgic thoughts. She poured the water over the tea leaves, adding milk and honey. She would drink this in bed. Perhaps it would calm her racing mind and the anxiety she had felt ever since her nephew had called from Vermont. They had found the secret room. They had found the dollhouse. Something must be done, and she must do it. But what?

As she made her way up the stairs to the tower where her master bedroom was located, Fiona decided to take one more peek into the attic to make sure she had completed her tasks. As she entered, she felt along the wall for the light switch that flooded the room with soft light from the old fixture hanging from the center of the ceiling. An attic it might be, but the space was quite beautiful and had commanding views of the property. It was one of her favorite places in the house. *It will make a fine bedroom for the next owner.* The thought made her frown. She stood by the window, looking out and sipping her tea.

Her thoughts drifted to the dollhouse. How long had it been safely hidden and out of harm's way? Walking to the far corner of the room, she looked at the boxes that she had packed as she considered the remaining inventory. Several old dining chairs sat in the corner as well as an old writing desk. *Who had used that desk last?* she wondered.

She sipped her tea. Did she remember using it as a young girl? She couldn't be sure. She realized that she had never inspected it for papers. She walked over and sat in front of the mahogany desk, running her fingers over the top. She opened the bottom drawer and saw that it was a good thing that she had done so because, in the drawer was a leather box.

"I guess I have more work to do up here tomorrow morning." As she stood, she grabbed the box and tucked it under her arm. She picked up her tea and walked back to her bedroom. Tossing the box onto her bed, she changed into her gown and finished off the last of the tea. She walked to the window and placed her hand on the radiator to feel the comforting heat, gazing out the window at the full moon sitting low on the horizon. Still not ready for bed, she glanced at the box at the foot of the bed. *What secrets might it hold?*

She crawled into bed and pulled the covers of her down comforter up to her chin, then sat up and pulled the box next to her. It was old, perhaps older than she could even imagine, and it was not in good condition. It was made of leather which was not only frayed by age and handling, but looked as though it might have been in water, or at least had water spilled on it. Leather straps held the lid in place. She gave the box a gentle shake, then pulled the straps off and lifted the lid.

The first thing she saw was even more worn than the box and looked like a diary. It, too, had a leather strap that held it shut. She could see tattered yellow pages protruding from the side. Carefully she opened the book to reveal a handwritten journal. She recognized the writing immediately as being penned by her mother. The diary had gone missing long ago. She had searched every inch of the castle looking for it but it seemed to have vanished, and she had nearly forgotten it existed.

"It can't be!" she said aloud.

Her eyes widened as she began to read. She opened a loose page that had been tucked into the front and opened it with trembling hands. "How is it possible? How did this letter—*this* letter written to me—find its way in here?" She read it in silence:

Dearest Fiona,

> *It makes me sad to write this letter of warning to you and even more sad to burden you with this task. Our family has a horrible secret that I have gone to great lengths to protect and contain. There is a dollhouse that was sent to our family cottage in Vermont. It is hidden away in a magical place for safekeeping. You are the only one that I am trusting with this information. There are other items that are hidden and shall remain hidden, even from you, for the*

*safety of our family now and for our future generations.
There is a dark power that we have unleashed. I will
not speak of it.*

*Dear Fiona, you must ensure that the dollhouse
remains hidden from your sister. She must never know
of its existence. I am so sorry to burden you with this.
She is not what she appears to be, and even she does not
know. I must leave you now. My dear, I am sorry to leave
you this way, but it is my hope that your father and I
have stopped something dreadful from happening.*

My love to you, always

"Oh, my, it has been so long since I read these words," she
whispered. Proceeding carefully, for she knew this to be a treasure,
she gently turned the pages, stopping as her hand touched a delicate
chain. She held the book open to reveal the necklace. She held it up
to the light.

"So, it's true. You exist. Oh, my. Oh, my! How have I never seen
this necklace before?"

Her first instinct was to call Abigail, but it was late. The woman
would be in bed and, in any case, what could she do at this time of
night? Fiona would make the call first thing in the morning.

All thoughts of sleep forgotten, Fiona spent the rest of the night
poring over the hundreds of pages in the journal that chronicled
the long-forgotten history of her family. What she read could not
possibly be true. But, deep in her gut, she knew it was.

She remembered the last conversation she had with her mother
on the very night that both her parents had disappeared. Tucked
inside her jewelry box she found the gilded hairpin that once
belonged to her mother and her grandmother. On their last night
together, her mother entrusted the hairpin to Fiona with a warning
and a promise. The memories were bittersweet, but it was time for

bravery. She placed the hairpin lovingly into her hair, styling a loose bun. "Mother, I trusted you then and I am trusting you now. I do not know how, but you said this hairpin would protect me when I need it most."

She made the call at first light. The phone rang six times before Abigail picked up, followed by a thud of the handset hitting the floor before she switched on her professional tone. "Good morning, ma'am. How are you this morning?"

"Abigail, this is going to be a busy day. I know this is your day off, but could you possibly come to the manor?"

"Just give me time to shower and dress and I'll be there."

Within the hour, Abigail arrived to learn that all the plans she had been working on for the past six months had changed. She found Fiona in the kitchen finishing another cup of tea and dressed as if she were attending an important meeting.

"Sit down," she waved to Abigail. "First thing, I want you to call the estate agent. The house is no longer for sale. First thing. Make the call."

"Right away." Abigail knew not to ask why, and she anticipated there was more.

"I am flying to America—Vermont—to see my nephew, his wife and," she stammered, "their daughter, Becky. I haven't packed, so please help me with that. I'd really like to go today if there's a flight you can get me on."

"I'll do it right away. Do you want me to come with you?"

"No, Abby, I need you to stay here, please. Once I get over there, I may have further instructions for you. I wouldn't ask if things were not urgent."

"I'm always happy to help with whatever you need. You know that."

CHAPTER 7

When the apple is ripe, it will fall.

—IRISH PROVERB

After helping her mother clean up the dinner dishes, Becky wanted to get back to her room. The mirror needed to be put someplace safe. She didn't want it near the dollhouse. The matching stone pattern that was identical to that collar gave her the creeps. She planned to hide it under the floor with the other mystery items—just to be safe. But when she got upstairs, she found Ginger straddled behind the dollhouse, her ears draped over the front, obscuring a section of its second floor. Her left rear leg was resting lightly on the roof with her right rear leg carrying all her weight. Her rump was in the air, and her tail was wagging wildly as she leaned over the house.

"Ginger, what is it?" Her eyes scanned the room looking for the mirror. "Where is the mirror, Ginger?"

Ginger's head popped out from the back of the house, and she lost her footing and flopped on her side and rolled, hitting the floor with a loud thud.

"Are you okay, Ginger?" She cradled Ginger's rear and hips and pulled her free. With only a fleeting glance at Becky, Ginger crawled back to the house, on her belly, and peered inside. Her tail wagged slowly. Becky crawled over to get a view of what Ginger was staring at.

"The mirror. Who put it inside?" Becky's heart raced. She reached to remove the mirror, but Ginger put her face up to block her hand. Becky slid back a few feet to observe.

A tiny shadow drifted slowly along the ceiling inside the dollhouse's second floor rooms. At first, Becky was unsure if it was coming from a light source outside the dollhouse. She closed the blinds and curtains in her room. She then noticed the soft glow coming from inside the house. She turned off all the lights in her bedroom except one lamp, and sat back down on the floor. Ginger continued to stare at the room where the mirror sat. More movement, this time on the first floor of the dollhouse, in the darkest section. The puppy and Becky saw the outline of something. Everything about Ginger's mannerisms spoke of fear, a fear that also touched Becky. But why? This was just a dollhouse, a plaything made of wood and textiles and little stones. It had no life of its own. *So what's making those shadows move? And, if they are shadows, shadows of what?*

Ginger moved closer, just inches, sniffing the floor. Becky reached over to put her hand on her dog. Together they waited. Something moved toward them, still mostly hidden in shadows. It had spots, colorful spots. It was furry, small, half the size of a ball of her mother's knitting yarn. Becky felt her throat closing and swallowed hard. She was holding her breath.

Ginger edged closer. Her tail was no longer wagging. Her body was stiff. The creature was almost visible now, and Becky could see kangaroo-like hind legs, disproportionately large. It bounced up and down, apparently staring at them.

Becky whispered, "You're not a mouse."

The creature's eyes locked on Ginger, ignoring Becky. It hopped forward, fully in view, attempting to exit the dollhouse, but fell backwards.

Becky dared a whisper. "Ginger, its mouth is moving. What is it trying to say? It looks like it is mouthing your name." Becky leaned forward as close as she dared to decipher the inaudible word that was being repeated. Ginger's ears perked up in recognition. Was she able to hear what the creature was saying? Ginger replied with a loud, "woof-woof" followed by a soulful howl.

The creature smiled, then took a second step forward, attempting again to exit the dollhouse, but this time something yanked it backwards. Its expression turned to surprise. There was something else inside the dollhouse with the creature. Becky could see the reflection of wings in the mirror.

Becky reached past Ginger and grabbed the mirror. It was unexpectedly hot, making her drop it, but she caught it before it hit the floor and pushed it away from the dollhouse like it was a tarantula. Catching her breath, she said, "This mirror has got to stay away from the dollhouse."

Feeling confident with the mystery creature contained inside the dollhouse, Becky turned away and searched for somewhere to place the mirror for safekeeping. *The box. Of course.* She grabbed it and put the mirror inside, using a tissue to keep her hands from touching it.

"This gives me the creeps, Ginger. The dollhouse gives me the creeps. Maybe I can convince Mom and Dad to send it to Scotland. Get it out of here."

It was getting late and tomorrow was a school day. Becky considered taking the dollhouse downstairs to get it out of her room, but there was something about that furry thing that didn't seem dangerous. She went to bed, and much to Ginger's surprise, Becky fell asleep as soon as her head hit the pillow.

Ginger lay awake, not feeling the least bit sleepy. In fact, she had never been more awake. Quietly, she crawled toward the house, sliding her paws along the hardwood floor channeling her hunting instincts. She pressed her nose against the dollhouse window, sniffing and peering inside, hoping to locate movement. Her wish was granted. A long shadow slid along the back wall of one of the rooms, and into a darkened corner. A slender gray figure emerged and took shape. For a moment she saw the outline of a tiny girl.

The figure drifted briefly out of the shadow. A cold burst of air flew from the inside of the dollhouse sending a shiver across Ginger's body, but she kept her eyes focused on the shadow girl. It had wings. Ginger's eyes narrowed and she stifled her instinct to bark. She held her jowls tightly shut.

A thud rumbled from another part of the dollhouse. It was strong enough that the floor under Ginger's front paws vibrated. A light moved sluggishly through the dollhouse and Ginger got a brief glimpse of the winged girl. Her eyes seemed filled with terror as she met Ginger's gaze. Their eyes locked. Another movement in the house.

Ginger looked away to locate the source of the sound. She looked back, and the girl was gone.

A cold current of air was filling the bedroom. Ginger glanced over at Becky to make sure she was still asleep. With each exhaled breath, mist blew from Becky's nose and mouth. How cold must a room be for that to happen? Ginger examined the dollhouse. It was dark, silent. A thin layer of ice had settled on its roof. Ginger backed up slowly, her rump bumping into the edge of Becky's bed. She could still feel the icy cold breeze blowing from inside the dollhouse. The force of the wind changed direction and started to pull the air back inside the house. Her ears blew toward the dollhouse, blocking her eyes. She felt her front legs being pulled forward in a direction she did not want to go—back into the dollhouse, against her will. She leaned back, fighting the relentless tug.

Running and jumping were not her specialties, but she was determined to get away. She had to get onto the bed, off the floor.

Somehow, she managed to leap sideways just enough to release herself. She bounded toward the bed, landing in a belly flop just short of her target. With another lunge, she got her front legs onto the edge of the bed as she clawed her way up the side. She tunneled her way toward Becky where she curled into a safe ball, nervously waiting for both of them to be pulled into the dollhouse abyss. The bed felt warm. The sun was rising. The room became quiet. They had survived the night

Ginger felt drained from her sleepless night on guard, so after breakfast she went outside to the front porch and fell into a deep sleep. She dreamed of swimming across a racing river. Above her head colorful creatures flew all around her. Some were diving and trying to bite her. The dream was intensely realistic. She felt her nose stinging from the attack and held her breath as she dove under the water to get away from the creatures. Each time she came up for air she was gasping. She dove deeper into the river, trying to retrieve something shiny at the bottom. Her legs jerked, and her nose wrinkled in aggressive expressions. She felt the pull of an invisible force that was working against her. As she struggled to reach the shoreline, she prepared to fight off the flying creatures. Her feet touched solid ground, but the soil disappeared under her feet, and she rolled down a steep, rocky cliff. She awoke with a jolt just in time to realize that she was falling off the front porch. Whimpering and panicked, she crashed into the hydrangea bush that bordered the front porch steps. Purple and blue petals flew in all directions as Ginger rolled clumsily onto the ground. Feeling dazed, she scrambled to her feet as she looked in horror at the hydrangea bush with its branches bent and broken. Using her nose, she shoved several of the largest branches back to the center and tried to dig around the bush to repair the damage.

She moaned. Thinking how much she did not want to get into trouble for damaging the family's beautiful flowers, she dashed into the yard in hopes of putting some distance between herself and the melee. After looking cautiously back toward the house to verify that nobody had heard anything, she decided to hang out in the yard for as long as possible before heading back inside. Her paws were a muddy mess. Twigs, leaves, and flower petals clung to her fur. She rolled on the ground using her hind legs to backstroke across the grass until she heard a fluttering sound next to her right ear. She jumped up, feeling alarmed and violently scratching her ear with her back leg, hoping to dislodge whatever was making that horrible sound.

A hitchhiking praying mantis crawled out from a twig that clung to Ginger's ears. She shook her head wildly back and forth, sending the mantis temporarily airborne. Fluttering in the turbulence, the bug crashed on the bridge of Ginger's nose before skidding to a stop on the tip. It dug its claw frantically into the soft tip as Ginger stifled a reflexive sneeze.

"What is the meaning of this?" demanded the mantis. "If I had a stinger, you'd be in trouble right now!"

Being a peacemaker, Ginger offered to return him to his resting place on the hydrangea, but the mantis continued to shout and bounce. His wings were fluttering so hard that Ginger's lashes bent backwards, and she squinted as if blown by a windstorm. Finally, the shouting stopped. The mantis paused to take a breath. "What do you have to say about this?"

With a warm smile, Ginger cleared her throat and gently spoke a heartfelt apology for disrupting his peaceful afternoon. She offered, "I'll be happy to return you to the garden and place you on the flower of your choice. What is your name?"

"Apology accepted." In a softer tone, the mantis said, "My name is Rothschild and I am—"

The sound of Becky and her mother approaching interrupted the conversation. Ginger had slept longer than she had realized, and Becky was home from school. As the two people got closer, Ginger wagged her tail enthusiastically to greet them, forgetting about her hitchhiker. Dried mud, twigs, leaves and flower petals flew in all directions.

Becky frowned and walked quickly toward Ginger with her hands up, covering her eyes. She bent down and stared at the top of Ginger's head.

"Will you look at that," her mom said, sounding amazed. "It's a giant praying mantis that hitched a ride on Ginger." They both came even closer, and the mantis stood frozen with its front legs stuck out in a pointing pose.

"I bet the mantis is giving Ginger a piece of its mind. Becky, would you put the poor thing back out on the grass? And Ginger needs to be cleaned up before she comes indoors. She's filthy!"

"No problem, Mom," Becky replied with a slight frown. She whispered to Ginger as she searched for a branch sturdy enough to transport the mantis. "What have you gotten into today?"

Rothschild, feeling relieved that he had escaped this near-death experience, thanked Ginger. "I am happy that we met. Come back out to the garden, *very soon*. We have a lot of things that I need to discuss with you. You see, I know something about the doll—"

Becky returned with a piece of cardboard and quickly brushed Rothschild off Ginger's nose. He slid down, headfirst, gently landing in the tall grass. "Well, that was rude," he exclaimed, trying to make sure that Ginger heard him. "Meet me back here! Tomorrow. We need to talk!"

Becky watched the mantis for a moment to make sure it landed safely before throwing a towel over Ginger to clean her paws. "You really are a mess. What have you been doing today? Come on, let's go back inside."

Rothschild watched as they disappeared inside.

CHAPTER 8

May your home always be too small to hold all your friends.

—IRISH PROVERB

As soon as Becky left for school the next morning, Ginger returned to the front yard. She had spent another sleepless night thinking about the strange events surrounding the dollhouse, and the secret room. Her encounter with the mantis added another layer of mystery. Had she heard him mention the dollhouse? Was it possible that the mantis was trying to tell her something? *I need to find that bug. . . what did he say his name was?* Ginger dashed outside toward the wildflower garden, sniffing the ground and hoping to pick up his scent.

"Why do I bother sniffing?" she mumbled, feeling hopeless. "My sniffer is defective, broken, useless." She stopped and her sadness faded into a tail-wagging epiphany. *I remember! Rothschild! That's his name! Rothschild!*

Filled with renewed confidence, Ginger eagerly circled the flowers, gently weaving between the purple coneflowers and lilacs to ensure that she did not trample them. Something caught her attention and she stopped, sniffing the air. There he was, crawling on a large goldenrod. The flower stem bowed under the weight of the mantis. Rothschild was perched on one of the more delicate flowers that adorned the top of the towering plant.

"Wow, I can't believe I found you," Ginger exclaimed!

"You found me? *I* found *you*. In fact, I've been right here in front of you this entire time. I can't believe you didn't see me. This is the fourth flower I had to crawl on just to get your attention. I've been hoping that we could finish our conversation that we started yesterday when I landed on your nose. You see, I'm a problem-solving praying mantis, and I happen to know that you need my services."

"What's a problem-solving praying mantis? What do you do? What kinds of problems do you solve? How are we able to talk to one another and understand each other?"

"You have a problem. I will fix it. It's that simple. I am not the only creature you are able to communicate with. There are more like me, more friends you will meet that you will be able to speak to and understand." The mantis's triangular head turned left, then right, then it froze, his eyes staring off in another direction.

Ginger cleared her throat and replied carefully, "Sounds like you would be a good friend to have, I guess."

Something about the mantis felt familiar, as if she had known him for a long time. She liked him, and she had a problem—maybe many problems—and she needed a problem solver. She considered how to bring up the dollhouse and the hidden room that gave her the creeps.

"So, introduce yourself to me," Rothschild said. "Tell me all about yourself." His tone was comforting and felt warm, inviting Ginger to sit by a fire and eat bacon. Ginger felt her stomach growl.

"Of course. My name is Ginger Miller and I am a full-blooded registered, from champion bloodlines, basset hound. I guard the yard, the house and the family, especially Becky and, really, I am a member of the family with certain rights that dogs do not normally get."

"Such as?"

Ginger looked round to make sure no one was listening. "I sleep in Becky's room," she whispered. "Usually on her bed, though her parents don't know that. I get table scraps all the time. I ride in the car, usually in the front seat; and I get to wear people clothes."

"People clothes? And that's a good thing? Well, I am glad you shared that with me. I certainly needed that information." This was delivered in a very strange tone. "Tell me about Becky."

Comfortable with her new friend, Ginger plopped down and told Rothschild all about how Becky found her in the chicken house when she was a puppy. She described how the two of them had become best friends, but she left out all the details of the dollhouse and the hidden room that gave her the creeps. Rothschild stared into Ginger's eyes, studying her. His head turned side to side processing the information. Ginger poured out her heart to Rothschild, as the mantis voiced an occasional, "Oh, yes, sounds important."

Ginger stopped talking. Rothschild's expression had changed.

"You did not bring up the dollhouse," the insect said.

The statement hung in the air. Ginger shivered with surprise and fear. "Why would I mention the dollhouse? What do you know about the dollhouse?"

The mantis stared at Ginger with his head cocked to one side and his front legs posed as if holding an invisible object. "You will be making a journey very soon. Think of it as an adventure." His voice trailed off as he looked off in the distance, toward the stream that bordered the far edge of the farm.

"An adventure? You mean go somewhere?"

"Isn't that what I said?"

"No, you don't understand, I can't. I might get lost."

The mantis's tone became much more demanding. "Weren't you listening to what I told you? You *will* be going."

"Yes, yes, I was listening, of course I was, but a couple things I failed to tell you. First of all, I have chronic stuffy nose syndrome, so I don't smell well and if I got lost, I would not be able to find my way back home. Second, my internal doggie directional compass. You might know it as a GPS. It was broken at birth. East, west, north, south—I don't know which way is up. If I lose sight of the top of the house chimney, I won't get back home. I could spend days—no, weeks—roaming, lost, hungry."

"No! You need to tell me what *you* know about the dollhouse. What is inside it? And what is inside the hidden room? Tell me now," the mantis demanded.

Panic gave way to anger and Ginger felt the hair on her back bristle up as she fought the urge to run inside the farmhouse.

Rothschild took a deep breath, sighed and then replied, "I have a friend who wants to meet you, and you are going to love him! Forget what I said about a journey. For now, at least."

"A friend? Who? Does he know something about the dollhouse?" Ginger felt her fear subsiding.

Rothschild replied in a gentle, patient tone. "He's been my friend for a long, long time. He is very wise. His name is Norm. I call him 'Norm the Nose,' but don't you call him that when you first meet him."

"Why do you call him Norm the Nose?"

"Norm is a giant snapping turtle, but much like you, he was born different. He has an enormous nose. What's even better, and one of the reasons I want you to meet him, is that he has a *great* sense of smell. He can smell for miles and miles. He can smell steaks cooking on another continent. Which is not much use to him as it happens, because he's a vegetarian. *A vegetarian turtle*. Not many of those around."

"Well, let's go meet him," Ginger said, with renewed enthusiasm.

"Not so fast, Ginger. Come back tomorrow morning, first thing. Meet me right here and I'll take you to Norm."

"That's a deal," said Ginger. "I really look forward to this. Thank you so much, Rothschild, thank you."

That evening after dinner, Becky went out to the garage and found an old tarp. She dusted it off and brought it up to her room. Ginger watched as she carefully spread it out beside the house.

"I've been thinking about this dollhouse," Becky said. "I think it would be best to get it out of my room if I can. At least for now. What do you think Ginger? Does that sound like a good idea?"

Ginger wagged her tail, bouncing clumsily off the bed and running over to grab a corner of the tarp to help straighten it.

"I'll take that as a *yes* from you! Thanks for the help, Ginger."

Becky leaned over to lift the corner of the house onto the tarp but met with resistance. The house seemed suddenly far heavier than it had been when she and her dad first brought it upstairs.

"All I need is to lift it a couple of inches to get it on this tarp. Why won't it budge?" She strained to lift it, trying to get a grip on the center of the structure, but it stayed where it was as though bolted to the floor. When she tried to pull it toward the tarp, it would not budge. She sat on the floor and used her legs to push it. No movement. Ginger watched helplessly. The house was going nowhere. Becky considered calling her father up to help. But, if the house was somehow magically glued to the floor, what would her parents do? Becky frowned, because the daughter of two scientists is brought up to believe that everything has a sensible explanation, but there was nothing sensible about this dollhouse. Had the time come for her to tell her parents about the furry creature living inside it? What about the objects hidden under the floor of her bedroom?

"If I show them the dollhouse that's now stuck to the floor, I will have to tell them about that furry creature that's inside and the hidden stash under my bedroom floor. If they get that stuff out it could trigger a repeat of whatever happened the night I found you, Ginger. I am not going to risk that. No. I am not going there." Ginger trotted over to the floorboards where the items were hidden and flopped down on top of them.

"I am glad you agree. You always understand me Ginger! Okay, plan B." She stared at the dollhouse. "I could cover it. But what would that do? Perhaps we'd better leave it for now. I think we can risk that the furry creature will leave us alone." She said to Ginger. Without further discussion Becky carefully rolled up the tarp and went downstairs to put it back where she'd found it.

When she got back to her room, she rummaged through her bookbag and started on her math homework. She wasn't going to look at the dollhouse at all.

It was another restless night for Ginger as she anxiously awaited the opportunity to meet Norm the Nose. As soon as Becky left for school, she raced to her doggie door in search of Rothschild. When Ginger got too enthusiastic, she would become very clumsy, so it was no surprise that she almost stepped on the mantis as she went dashing out for their meeting. Panicked and waving his arms wildly, he yelled, "Watch out, for heaven's sake! I'm sitting here plain as day, slow down, you're going to run me over!"

Ginger put on the brakes as quickly as she could, but bassett hounds don't stop or change direction with ease. Attempting at the last moment to avoid squashing her new friend, Ginger sat down hard and thudded to a stop, digging a small trench in the ground which, unfortunately, Rothchild fell into.

Brushing off, he climbed on the puppy's tail, mumbling under his breath. "What am I getting myself into? This hound is going to be the death of me."

Ginger sheepishly apologized to Rothschild. "Whew, that was a close one. I'm so glad I didn't land on you!" She paused for another moment to make sure he was okay, and then trotted toward the stream for what she hoped would be answers about what was living in the dollhouse and what danger it might pose.

As she approached the stream and saw Norm sitting on a large rock, apparently waiting for her, she whispered, "How did I miss him all those times I visited the stream? He's huge." As they came closer, she saw the turtle's giant hooked beak and realized he could snap the tip of her nose off with one bite. She felt relieved they had never met before and welcomed a friendly introduction from Rothschild.

Norm's hook glistened in the sun like a giant dagger ready for battle; a dagger that could do serious damage. Ginger's wobbly legs threatened to collapse under her weight. A feeling of danger and dread washed over her. She felt the urge to run home. She considered some possible excuses. She had skipped breakfast that morning and needed to eat? Today was bath day? Maybe even a vet appointment that she had forgotten about? She slowed her trot to a trudge, and then stopped far enough from the snapping turtle that it was impossible for him to reach her.

Rothschild scrambled up her back. "Why are you stopping? Come on, Norm wants to meet you."

"You didn't tell me how scary he looks. That hook. No, I don't think this is a good idea." Ginger planted her butt on the ground, refusing to move.

"*It . . . will . . . be . . . fine.* You are being ridiculous. Trust me. You're going to like Norm. A lot. You need to hear the story about how we met. It is so funny."

Ginger kept her eyes on the turtle. She could see a blue shimmer on the tip of his giant hook. As she reassessed his appearance, the blue sparkles made him seem a little less intimidating, and maybe even friendly. Norm broke her trance. "Are you coming or not? I've been waiting here to meet you, and my shell is drying out like a piece of cowhide."

The image made Ginger laugh and she trotted happily to the water's edge. "I'm sorry. Shall I splash some water on you?"

With a giant splash, Norm did a turtle belly flop into the stream and swam gracefully to where Ginger stood. Ginger felt relieved when she saw his giant face rise grinning from the water. "I'm happy to meet you, Ginger. Let's get comfortable. We have a lot to talk about."

Remembering that Rothschild had said his first meeting with Norm had been funny, Ginger asked, "Tell me how you met Rothschild?"

"Poor Rothschild. I think he thought it was the end for him. It was an autumn day, unusually warm for the time of year, and I was basking in the sun, enjoying those last few days of warmth. I'll tell you the truth: I was asleep. I was dreaming of apples falling from the sky when I felt something like a feather tickling the end of my nose. It made me sneeze. And that was Rothschild. He'd accidentally fallen off a branch hanging over my rock. He thought he was going to be my lunch. You should have heard him!"

Rothschild butted in. "As you can see, I'm large for a praying mantis, but however large a praying mantis might be, it knows that turtles are bigger. And they like to eat us. And this was the biggest turtle I'd ever set eyes on. But I'm not just big for a mantis, I'm also clever for a mantis and I think fast, so I shouted, 'Don't even think about it. I taste very bitter.' That was intended to deter him because, who wants a bitter lunch?"

"Now, as it happens, I don't eat bugs," said Norman, interrupting, "but I wanted to have some fun so I shouted back, 'Don't worry about me. It's that blue jay over there, the one eyeing you right now. That's who you need to worry about.' You should have seen the look on Rothschild's face! But I didn't expect him to freak out quite as wildly as he did. He ducked into the water and started doing the backstroke, but he bumped his head on a stone. I felt bad about it." Norm's laugh suggested he hadn't felt as bad as all that.

Rothschild said, "There was no blue jay. And after Norm explained he was a vegetarian and wouldn't eat a bug if his life depended on it, well, that was the start of a beautiful friendship."

"Anyways," said Norm, "amusing though this is, it isn't what I want to talk to you about, Ginger. Rothschild and I have passed many hours watching you and Becky on your visits to the stream."

"But we never saw you!" Ginger said.

"You weren't intended to. When I was very young, one of my brothers was scooped up by a little boy and put into a big glass bowl. We had one heck of a job rescuing him, and I was determined to never let that happen to me. So, Rothschild and I came to an arrangement. If Becky got too close, Rothschild would freeze in a funny pose, like a statue. That was my signal to swim out into the deeper part of the stream."

It was a fun memory, but Norm was right; this was not why they needed to meet with Ginger. That had to do with the dollhouse, and the very thought took all ideas of happy laughter from Rothschild's mind.

"It is time for us to discuss the problem. Enough with our stroll down memory lane. We need to tell Ginger about the strange things that are happening, *over there*."

Ginger looked where Rothschild pointed. On the far side of the pond she could see the stream spilling over rocks that bordered the pond's deeper banks. The water flowed lazily through the grassy meadow, then disappeared into the woods. Her eyes locked on the woods. The dark woods where no sunlight entered.

"Yes," said Norm. "I agree. Ginger, sit, and let us tell you what we know. Do you see that line of trees that Rothschild pointed to?"

Ginger locked her eyes on Norm and slowly nodded.

"Those woods are creeping closer," Norm said. "They're crowding in on us. Moving closer to the meadow and your house."

Ginger replayed in her mind the words *crowding in . . . moving closer . . . your house* as she tried to control her breathing. She felt her heart begin to race.

Norm continued, speaking slowly. "I have the most powerful sense of smell you can imagine. I can smell anything. The nicest smell around these parts is the Millers' weekly lasagna. Especially the scent of basil and tomatoes."

"Yuck," said Ginger. "I hate tomatoes. I love bacon, though. My sense of smell is dreadful, but even I can smell bacon when someone is cooking it."

"Well," Norm continued, "I can smell something now. Something is wrong. It started out faint, but now the scent is strong and close."

Ginger made no attempt to sniff the air. Norm might be right and he might be wrong, but a nose as useless as hers wasn't going to find the answer. Norm waited to see if she understood. He waited for her first question, but all he heard was silence. Rothschild looked as though he was about to speak, but Norm shot him a stern glance. Ginger searched her mind and sifted through the questions and fears that weighed on her. She felt dizzy, and blinked to clear her vision. *Why am I panicking?* she thought. *I am here, close to my home and safe.*

"When did this start?" She managed to ease the question out without crying.

And there it was. The question that Norm was not sure he wanted to answer. "It started the night you arrived, Ginger."

Ginger's fur stiffened. She couldn't have run away if she tried because her legs had gone wobbly. Gently, Rothschild asked, "Do you remember the night you arrived here?"

Ginger searched her mind carefully before she spoke. "I don't remember much. Someone dropped me off when I was a puppy. It was a cold night and they left me in the chicken house. That is where Becky found me."

Norm and Rothschild exchanged glances. "What else do you remember?"

"That's all. Becky brought me inside and I became a member of the family. That's all. That's all there is."

"Ginger, I'm going to be honest with you," Norm said. "First of all, I'm not sure how much more you can handle right now. Second, there are things I don't remember, either, because it wasn't only you that something happened to. Something happened to me as well. The night you arrived, a bright glowing light appeared inside that chicken house. It started low but grew brighter. Becky saw the light. Did you ever hear her mention it?"

Ginger shook her head motioning no.

"It was after that night that the strange smell started, and the woods began to move and grow darker. We don't think you caused it, but you are somehow connected to it."

Norm and Rothschild both saw the terror in Ginger's eyes as she processed the information.

Darkness invaded the sky and they looked up to see that a large shadowy winged figure had blocked the sun. It flew slowly over the tree line. The sun was beginning to set, its position low in the sky that said the trio had been together most of the day. Ginger eased her question out in a whisper as she looked skyward. "What *is* that?"

Norm started to answer and then stopped. He seemed unable to speak at all until Rothschild's anxious voice pulled him from his trance. "Are you all right? What happened?"

Norm shuddered. Ginger had never seen a turtle shake before. Brave as Norm undoubtedly was, something had spooked him badly. Finally, the shaking came to an end and Norm said, "I was transported far from here. By what, by whom, I have no idea. I stood on the edge of a high cliff. There was an icy wind. A woman was speaking to me, but I couldn't make out what she was saying over the sound of the wind and the roaring of snow blowing all around me. That thing that just flew over the trees. Have either of you seen it before?"

Ginger indicated with a slow nod that she had not seen this strange bird thing before. But Rothschild was silent.

CHAPTER 9

A certain darkness is needed to see the stars.

—OSHO

Norm and Ginger wanted to know whether Rothschild had ever seen the winged creature before. And, of course, he had, and he remembered that the winged creature said that threatening things would be happening. After that warning, threatening things did indeed start to happen. The winged creature said that if the threatening things weren't dealt with in exactly the right way, the results would be ruinous. If the creature was there to help, who was she there to give help to? Rothschild and his friends? Or those others?

Sharing this warning with Norm and Ginger would relieve Rothschild of the burden of carrying this secret alone, and it would give Norm a chance to sort things out and make some sensible suggestions. Rothschild wasn't one to kid himself, and he knew that Norm's brain operated on a higher level than his own.

As he weighed whether to share his secret, Rothschild remembered something else the winged creature had told him: "You must tell no one about this conversation. Do you understand,

Rothschild? If you break that instruction, I will know. And I will not be happy with you."

So what was Rothschild to do? He didn't want Norm to be unhappy with him, but he wanted even less for the unhappiness to be felt by the winged creature. Norm was a vegetarian turtle. He wouldn't eat a praying mantis. Was that also true of the winged creature? Rothschild didn't want to find out. He would tell the truth without breaking his promise.

He would change the subject. "Listen, you two. I know people, and I've been asking around, and my people tell me that something is seriously wrong. Someone bad is coming and they mean to do us all harm, and that means Becky and your family, Ginger."

Norm looked perplexed. "You know people? *What people?* And why have you never mentioned this before?"

"Like I said, Norm, I know people, and what I am hearing is that there's something wrong at the Millers' house and it's all about to blow up."

A horrified Ginger shouted, "Blow up?"

"Not like that. Not like a bomb. But it's something we have to deal with."

"Well," said Norm, "I don't think you're telling us anything we don't already know, but I do agree, something is very wrong and we are going to have to investigate. But I don't think Ginger is up for it. Not yet, anyway."

"Well," said Rothschild, "she'd better get up for it, because I've been told by a very reliable source that something extremely unpleasant is going to be calling on Ginger very soon."

Norm said, "I wonder if that's the cotton candy aroma I've been smelling recently."

"Aha!" shouted Rothschild. "You *do* know more than you've been saying!" He rubbed his front legs together as if to say, "I knew it!" This was all going better than he could have expected; Norm was accepting his story about knowing people.

"All I'm saying is that this is not the time for Ginger. She is not ready," Norm said.

"That's right," said Ginger. "Let's wait, like Norm says. Rothschild, you are scaring me. I did not make friends with the two of you so I could be kidnapped and taken into those woods. I'd die of fright if nothing else killed me first. In fact, I have to be back home. It's late, and I should be there waiting for Becky. That's my job. It's what I do. You can tell these people you know that I want nothing to do with them."

After she'd gone home, Norm said, "You need to be more careful what you say in front of Ginger, Rothschild. She's had a sheltered upbringing. She goes into a warm house every evening and sleeps on Becky's bed. She doesn't have to deal with the outdoors the way we do."

Rothschild looked towards the woods. The sun was barely visible now through the trees, but as she and Norm watched, the darkness moved and took shape. Large black wings stretched, too large to be any bird either of them had ever seen. Just for a moment in the gathering darkness, its eyes flashed red. Norm looked in the direction where Ginger had gone and said, "Do you think Ginger saw that?"

"I'm sure she did. And I'm sure she realized those eyes were staring at her."

"Whenever she's not in the house, Rothschild, it's your job to know where she is. I'm counting on you. Don't let her out of your sight."

Rothschild shuddered. That was a heck of a responsibility. He wished now that he'd told the truth about his meeting with the winged creature instead of inventing a lot of nonsense about "knowing people."

Becky's father was a confident, level-headed scientist. Jeff Miller prided himself on seeking facts rather than chasing shadows or half-truths. Staying grounded had served him well in his career as a historical researcher. Unfortunately, some of his recent discoveries had put his pragmatic foundations to the test and had cost him his job and most likely his reputation. He wanted to shield Becky from as much of it as possible. The discovery of the secret room turned out to be a wellspring of hidden family secrets, including a book that contained family genealogy connecting his ancestors to sorcery. He felt himself being pulled headfirst down a path that felt more like mythology than science.

Rachel Miller shared her husband's scientific, factual philosophy. She had a prove-it-to-me outlook that always kept her eyes firmly on what could be tested, authenticated and replicated. Her reaction to the diary was much more subdued, thinking it read like a work of fiction and not a historical relic of family genealogy. "I know it's been a hard year for us, but surely you can't, even for a minute, entertain that what is written in this diary could have *ever* happened to our family!" she implored her husband. "Please tell me that you know this is fiction. We don't even know for sure who wrote it."

"No. We don't. But the room. This place. I can't describe it, but it feels significant to me. That's why I'm setting up a lab. In that room. I want to do an archaeological dig."

"In the center of our house? After all we've been through? What exactly did Fiona say?"

Jeff looked away for a moment, as if he intended to do something he had never done in all the time they had known each other— mislead Rachel. But honesty got the better of him, as in the end it always did.

"Aunt Fiona said she was putting her manor house up for sale. She said she was sorry that Becky would not see it while it was still in the family. But then—"

"When you mentioned the hidden room and especially the dollhouse?"

"Yes. Then. Her tone changed. And when I told her we'd unpacked the dollhouse and it was in Becky's room, she became upset. I asked her what was wrong with the dollhouse and she didn't answer me quite as squarely as I'd have hoped. She said there was nothing inside the dollhouse that would harm Becky. And then she said she was dropping everything, changing all her plans, and coming here."

When they got together to eat that evening, seeing Ginger, curled into a ball under the table with her ears wrapped around her head, Becky's father said, "Is Ginger all right?"

Becky replied with a frown, "She's been noticeably quiet ever since I got home from school, which is very strange for her. And she's stayed close to me. Almost as though she was scared of something."

"Maybe she ate too much. Who's been sneaking Ginger extra bacon?"

Becky's mother asked with that face that Becky had come to recognize as the one she wore when she wanted to cheer up the atmosphere. She continued, "We're going to have a visitor. Your Great Aunt Fiona is flying here from Scotland."

It worked, because Becky was always pleased to see visitors, and the idea of meeting a great aunt she hadn't even known existed a few days ago was exciting. She looked at her father.

"Tell me about her."

"Well, I haven't seen her since I was about your age. My parents took me to Aberdeenshire for a visit."

"Aberdeenshire?"

"That's where she lives. It's a region of Scotland. It's what they call a county, although their counties aren't the same as our counties. A county there is more like a state here, only much smaller than most American states. Actually, not that much smaller than this one we're living in now, when I come to think about it. And the house Aunt Fiona lives in is something else. Almost like a fairytale. Like a castle. I don't remember all that much, but I do remember a hidden staircase, and the master bedroom was in a tall tower. The upper rooms in that tower have beautiful arched windows, as big as a cathedral, where you can see for miles. I wish we'd taken you to visit. Turns out, she is selling it."

"The dollhouse is almost a perfect match of our house except for the tower," said Becky. "Does Aunt Fiona's tower look anything like the one that is on the dollhouse?"

"Yes," said her father. "Yes. I hadn't thought of it until you mentioned it, but you're right. It does."

"What is your aunt like?" Becky asked.

"It's been a long time, but I remember feeling like she was royalty. She was very warm, but very formal. She was a lot younger then, of course, so she might have changed by now. She had long auburn hair that she wore in a ponytail, and she always wore a dress."

Becky's mother asked, "Did she ever marry?"

"No. She never married. We didn't keep up with the family in Scotland. We moved here to the States when I was still a baby, and that visit was the only time we went back. My parents rarely spoke about the family we left behind. I actually have another aunt in Ireland. Your mother mentioned her the other day, and that's the first time I've thought about family in Ireland since I was a boy."

"I can't wait to meet Great Aunt Fiona. I wonder what she will tell us about the dollhouse?"

CHAPTER 10

However long the day, the evening will come.

—IRISH PROVERB

Her bags packed, Fiona stood in her bedroom reading the diary, trying to convince herself that what she had read was fairytale fiction. Now, what to make of the discovery of the dollhouse in Vermont? She considered tucking the diary into her handbag to bring with her, but after reflecting on all the things she had read, she decided to put it back where she'd found it, for safekeeping. It might be best to keep it far away from the dollhouse, or anyone else for that matter.

She held the delicate necklace up to the light and examined it. Four beautiful stones in a setting of delicate, golden conjoined flowers. One stone was clear like a diamond, another blue and most likely a sapphire, then a red ruby and finally an emerald. In the center was a round black stone that she believed to be an onyx. She put the necklace in a small velvet-lined jewelry box and placed it with the diary. Then she reached inside the leather box and picked up an antique lock made of glass, which she tucked carefully into her handbag. The items that remained were secured inside a cotton bag and she returned them to the safety of the leather box.

The phone rang, startling her. She hoped Abigail would answer it for her, but the ringing continued. She lifted the receiver and said, "Hello."

The voice at the other end was cold and hostile. "Don't you dare think about taking that lock and getting it anywhere near the dollhouse."

"Catriona? Where are you calling from? And how did you know about the lock?"

"Don't do it, Fiona. You have no idea what you're playing with. I know about the lock the same way I know about the diary, the box and the necklace. You only had to touch that necklace and I knew. You've read the diary, haven't you? Haven't you?"

"Yes. I have."

"That diary is full of lies. You are being deceived. Leave it alone. We have to meet. There's more you need to see. You don't have what you think you have."

Fiona hung up. How could her sister possibly have known what she was touching? She grabbed her belongings and called for Abigail to bring the car to the door. As they were loading it, she had the strangest sense of being observed. She said, "Do you see anyone watching us?"

Abigail shook her head.

The disturbing call from Catriona created a sense of urgency in Fiona.

"We have lots of time before check-in," Abigail said. "We don't really need to leave for another hour."

"Perhaps. But let's go now anyway."

During the ride to the airport, Fiona thought about everything she'd read in the diary and about the very unpleasant call from Catriona. Perhaps she should forget about it, go home, make everything go back to the way it had been before she read the diary and found that necklace. Before she knew. This was turning into a nightmare, a nightmare five hundred years in the making. Perhaps she should stay out of it and let whatever happens happen.

Or maybe, instead of going to America, she should fly to Ireland. Meet her sister and hear what she had to say. She thought about the letter from her mother, the letter that had contributed to the longstanding rift between her and Catriona. But nothing positive would come from her speaking with Catriona again. *No. America it will be.*

When they reached the airport, she handed Abigail a sealed folder. "I'm sure everything is going to be fine. But if something should happen to me, or if you can't reach me for an extended time, open this and follow the instructions inside."

Abigail looked shaken. "Are you sure you don't want to wait and let me come with you?"

"Abby, there's lots to keep you busy here. I'll be fine. No need to worry. I'm going to sit in the lounge until takeoff. You go now and get on with what you were doing before I interrupted your day off."

It was almost three hours later, so early had she been for her flight, that Fiona finally boarded the aircraft. As the doors were about to close, a last-minute passenger came on board juggling several boxes and with a number of maps under her arm. Passing down the aisle, she made eye contact with Fiona before taking her seat across the aisle. Fiona noticed a strange pendant on the girl's neck.

"What an interesting necklace. What kind of design is inscribed?"

"It has been in my family for a long time. It is called a celestial navigator. With just the sun or moon as a guide, I can find any place in the world." She stared at Fiona, unblinking, and with her smile fading, she added, "I almost arrived too late. That would have been bad." She closed her eyes and turned her face away from Fiona.

Ginger was waiting in the kitchen for the family to return home from picking up Great Aunt Fiona at the airport. All morning Becky had talked with Ginger about Aunt Fiona and how happy she was to meet her relative from Scotland, especially because of her knowledge about the dollhouse. But Ginger wasn't happy about it at all. Maybe Aunt Fiona is nice and maybe she isn't so nice. She did not think it to be a good idea to trust anyone who had anything to do with the dollhouse.

The puppy heard the car in the distance as it made the turn from the main highway onto the dirt driveway leading to the farmhouse. Ginger jumped from the bed set up in the kitchen as her daytime napping spot, trotted to the window overlooking the front yard, and waited for the first signs of the car. As it made its slow way up the winding driveway, Ginger's tail swished with recognition, wagging faster and faster as they got closer. By the time she heard the car enter the garage she was in full-blown happy dance mode. She raced to the door, tongue wagging and ears dragging the ground as she maneuvered around the corner into the mud room.

She listened, attempting patience, to the chitter chatter and laughter as they approached the door. Ginger heard Becky tell Aunt Fiona that she was going to love her dog, Ginger. This caused even more excitement. When the door opened, Ginger catapulted towards Aunt Fiona with her front legs airborne and waving as she tried to balance against Fiona's hip. After a second or two Ginger's body made contact against Fiona with an ungraceful bounce.

"You poor dear," Fiona said as she leaned over to pet Ginger. She enthusiastically rubbed the basset hound behind her long ears and scratched her tummy. "She is a sweet girl, Becky. I can see why you love her so much."

After the exuberant greeting, Ginger felt a little better about Fiona and settled back down on her day bed to observe.

During dinner, Ginger stayed in the kitchen listening to Fiona tell Becky about Scotland, especially about the castle where she lived. Becky told Aunt Fiona how much she wanted to visit.

"I think that would be a fabulous idea. When is your next school break?" She looked towards Becky's parents. "She could fly to see me. I would meet her at the airport, of course. We would have a grand time."

Ginger felt her stomach tighten. She wasn't feeling so well, so she went upstairs to Becky's room and curled up on her blanket. The idea of Becky visiting Scotland made Ginger very uneasy. She looked at the dollhouse that sat in the dark corner of the room. She heard footsteps approaching. Although she felt suspicious of Fiona, Ginger had been willing to give her the benefit of the doubt. Perhaps she didn't know anything about bad things inside the dollhouse. But that willingness was about to come to an end.

Fiona walked quietly into the bedroom. Ginger thought about running over to greet her, but instead remained hidden in the corner, watching. Most of the lights were off except a small nightlight, and Fiona left them off as she tiptoed to the dollhouse. Ginger watched as she knelt in front of the house staring into the windows. She tapped on the front door. She whispered, "Anyone home?" and then said it again, but this time louder. "Anyone home?"

Ginger felt a cold sensation, and things did not improve when Fiona took a small flashlight out of her purse and shined it in the dollhouse, methodically moving from room to room. There wasn't any doubt in Ginger's mind that Fiona was looking for something. Or someone? She shone the light on every space and dark corner, pausing in each room before moving to the next space.

"Where are you?" Her voice trembled. Then Becky called from downstairs, "Aunt Fiona, would you like dessert?"

"Oh, yes, please. I'll be right down." Under her breath, she murmured, "I really must find you. Where are you hiding?"

Ginger could hear furniture being moved around, and tried to get a better view, but she did not want to risk being detected. Then

Becky came into the room. "Oh, Aunt Fiona, I'm sorry. I should have brought you up to see the dollhouse earlier."

Fiona was taken by surprise and let out a squeal. Ginger ducked behind Becky's bed, anxious not to be seen. "My dear," said Fiona. "You scared me." She stood and straightened her skirt. Ginger waited to hear her explanation, but none came.

Becky said, "It's a lovely dollhouse. It's amazing that it was hidden in that old walled-off room. What was it doing in there?"

"I'm glad you like it," said Fiona. "It's especially important that you take good care of it. This house is very old." She cleared her throat. "There should be a key. Have you seen the key?"

Becky wrinkled her forehead. "What does it look like? I never thought about it having a key because the house is open, and I did not need a key to put furniture inside."

Fiona smiled. Ginger didn't like that smile at all. She thought it was the kind of smile that a simple, trusting person like Becky might think was genuine, but Ginger knew better.

Fiona said, "It looks like a key that might fit into the front door of a dollhouse."

Becky laughed. "Of course! But I haven't seen one."

Fiona gestured that Becky should move closer to the dollhouse. She pointed at the front door. "You see that this front door actually has a lock? There is an important key that goes right here. We need to find it. Think really hard."

Ginger watched Becky closely. She knew all of Becky's moods, so she could tell that Becky was troubled. Ginger wanted to know why Fiona was asking about a key for a dollhouse abandoned long ago in an old sealed room, and now she knew that Becky was wondering exactly the same thing. It was time for Ginger to come out of hiding and show whose side she was on. She trotted across the floor and stood between Becky and Fiona. Her tail didn't budge an inch. Becky put her arms around Ginger and hugged her.

"I'm sorry, Aunt Fiona, I haven't seen a key. I don't think it was in the house. Perhaps it was lost when whoever put it in the hidden room packed it away." Becky replied.

Fiona glared at Becky. "No, it is not misplaced. It must be here." Then she seemed to realize she was being too forceful. "Maybe we can look tomorrow. We won't worry about it tonight, but tomorrow, first thing, we need to search everywhere to find the key."

She walked past Ginger without a glance and put her arm around Becky. "Let's go have some sweet."

Sweet? thought Ginger. *Is that what people in Scotland call dessert?*

"Come on, Ginger, let's have a treat," Becky patted her legs encouraging Ginger to follow, and the three went downstairs.

After dessert, Becky helped her mom clean up the kitchen. Fiona walked over to Ginger and sat down beside her, stroking Ginger's ears. She leaned over and whispered, "What do you know about the dollhouse? Are you going to help me, or get in my way?"

Ginger stared back at her, pretending not to understand and gently wagging her tail, watching Fiona as she got up and disappeared from the kitchen. "I'm exhausted from traveling. I hope you don't mind if I head up to bed early."

Ginger did not sleep well that night. Fiona gave her the creeps. What was Fiona willing to do to get the key? And why did she want it? Was Becky as afraid of Fiona as she was? Ginger was convinced that Fiona's apparent niceness was an act, and that they were in danger. She pulled her dog blanket over to the dollhouse. If anything moved inside, she would know about it; if Fiona came near it during the night, she would know about that, too. For hours she stared at the house. There was no sound.

Ginger was feeling so tired. She struggled to keep her eyes open, but they felt so heavy. Fighting sleep, she smelled something. *But I have a terrible sense of smell. This is so strange. Is that a sweet smell? Yes, so sweet. What is that smell?* She couldn't keep her eyes open. Maybe she was dreaming. She fought to stay awake, but as her eyes closed, she thought she saw a light flash inside the dollhouse, like a light switch had been turned on. Then she was asleep.

Next morning, Ginger woke to the sensation of cold air stinging her nose. She forced open her eyes and peered toward the window, staring out at the stream of sunlight. *Is it morning already?* Feeling groggy, she got to her feet, stretching and yawning. A current of cold air hugged the floor but she felt a warm breeze blowing from inside the dollhouse. She shook, ears to tail, twisting back and forth, ending with her tail. Becky's bed was empty and her covers rumpled. Ginger had overslept. She hoped she hadn't missed breakfast, which on Saturdays was pancakes. With a final stretch she stepped out of her dog bed then, puzzled, thought, *How did I get on my dog bed? I slept by the dollhouse.*

She went to the hallway. It felt so cold in the house. Before going downstairs she stopped to listen for the normal family breakfast sounds, but all she heard was silence. Why hadn't Becky awakened her to help feed the chickens? Unease was growing. Something was wrong. It was so cold in the house, and too quiet.

As she entered the hallway, the temperature fell abruptly. A dusting of snow covered the carpet and the walls glowed blue-white with an eerie, icy sheen as if they'd been hosed down in the subzero winter air. She needed to find everyone. They should be in the kitchen. She raced to the stairs, but her feet slipped on an ice-covered step midway down and she tumbled two steps before finding her footing and balance. She sailed over the last few stairs and belly flopped, skidding across the cold kitchen floor.

A thin layer of ice crystals crunched under her paws, and white vapor from her warm breath circled around her head as she walked slowly towards a scene she could not comprehend. Becky's parents were motionless, frozen in a glacial grip. Her dad was seated at the table with his coffee cup pressed against his lips, and in his left hand the newspaper was folded as he prepared to read the morning headlines. Mom was by the stove holding a mixing bowl, smiling.

Whatever this was, they did not see it coming. *Where is Becky?* Ginger started barking furiously, as loud as she had ever barked in her life, hoping that the sound would somehow break them from the icy grip holding them prisoners. In another attempt to break them free, she ran over and put her paws on Jeff's lap. He did not move or change his expression. He did not blink. She nudged his hand and felt the cold, icy dampness. No response. She ran over to Mom, barking and tugging at her slippers. No response. She raced through the entire first floor, looking in each room barking, howling and whining.

Ginger went back up the stairs to Becky's room. Feeling panic rise, she raced to the dollhouse in breathless desperation, panting. *What is going on?*

There, beside the dollhouse, she found the only warm spot. The area glowed with yellow light that felt like a small space heater. Ice crystals that covered all the other surfaces throughout the house could not invade this corner of Becky's room.

Ginger felt the panic melting and, in its place, clarity. She had to find Norm. He would help her track down Becky. She raced down the icy stairs again, leaping over the bottom three steps, and this time landing squarely on her hind legs as she slid toward the frozen doggie door. She bolted down the porch stairs skidding to an abrupt stop beside the flower bed.

Waiting at the bottom of the stairs were Norm, Rothschild, and a giant flying bug she had never seen before. "Norm, something terrible has happened," she cried. "Fiona has done something bad to Mom and Dad and she has taken Becky. We must do something. Now! They're frozen in there." Panting, she put her front paws on the steps and looked back to see if Norm was coming. Then she remembered, he could not get up those steps.

Norm spoke calmly. "Ginger, we're going to help. It's going to be okay."

"Do you know where Becky is? How do we unfreeze them? What is going on?" Ginger breathlessly fired the questions without pausing for a response.

Norm walked over to Ginger and reassured her. "You are going back inside. But first there is someone you need to meet. This is Blaze. He is coming with us."

Ginger looked up at the giant dragonfly hovering just above her head.

"He is going to be helping us now. You're not alone. Blaze will go back inside with you. We need to hurry." Norm turned his face up and sniffed the air. His nose was glowing a fiery golden red.

Blaze flew lower, near to Ginger's face. "Pan is in there. We need to get Pan."

Ginger, still reeling, whispered, "Pan? Who is Pan?"

CHAPTER 11

*May you never forget what is worth remembering
or remember what is best forgotten.*

—IRISH PROVERB

S now and ice had covered the farmhouse grounds. Carefully, Ginger climbed the ice-covered porch steps with Blaze flying above her head. Before they entered through the dog door, Blaze hovered low in front of Ginger's face to get her attention.

"We need to get in and get out of here fast. Norm and I are not sure who caused this to happen. We don't think they are still here, but that doesn't mean it's safe."

"What about Becky's parents?" Ginger whispered.

"The best thing we can do for them now is to go after the key and find Becky."

"Oh, thank heaven you know about the key."

"We don't have time for this now. Let's get upstairs." Blaze flew ahead through the dog door that was being pushed ajar by the growing avalanche of ice. The temperature in the house had continued to plummet. The walls were hidden under layers of ice that glistened eerily in the blue- white gloom. Ginger waded through deep snow as they made their way to the stairs, which were mostly covered by the blizzard. She trudged upward keeping her eyes focused on the soft glow coming from the second floor. When they arrived at Becky's room the door was closed. Ginger gave it a firm nudge, but it would not open. The air was frigid, and the dampness created minuscule ice droplets that drifted all around them.

"I can't get the door open. How will we get inside?"

Blaze disappeared through the keyhole.

The door opened a few inches, and Ginger could see inside. The room was warm and there was no snow or ice. Standing next to the house she saw the furry, spotted creature. Blaze hovered over the dollhouse, which was illuminated from the inside with twinkling white and yellow lights. When Ginger was safely inside the room, the door closed. The pup approached cautiously, keeping her eyes fixed on the creature, wondering if it was the cause of all this chaos or if it would be the helper she desperately needed. It was so beautiful, but tiny, no larger than a ball of yarn. It had white fur like a fluffy cotton ball with small spots like a leopard that had been dipped in neon rainbow-colored paint. It had powerful hind legs that looked like a rabbit's and it stood staring at her, bouncing.

Blaze landed on the roof of the dollhouse. Ginger walked over and sat. "Who did this? Do you know where Becky is?"

"We need to get Pan out of here. We can talk in a safe location. Pan, get whatever you need and then we'll leave. Sorry, Ginger let me introduce you. This is Pan."

Pan disappeared into the house and reappeared. He looked at Ginger, then held out his arm to touch her paw. "Close your eyes."

Ginger slammed her eyes shut, no time to question. She felt weightless and then a sensation of being pulled through a tight tunnel. The air was cold. Pounding snow hit her face, stinging her ears, and her lashes felt frozen shut as she tried to open her eyes. She struggled to breathe but no air would enter her lungs. And then, heat pressed against her fur and she felt the warm air move in and out of her lungs. The ice melted from her fur and lashes and she felt the familiar softness of grass under her feet. She heard Norm speak, "Ginger, open your eyes."

She was at the stream with Norm, Rothschild, Blaze and Pan. She looked back at the farmhouse, now blanketed in ice and snow. The brick chimney was partly visible, but she could see, even from this distance, that the farmhouse was under a wintry attack. The exterior walls dripped with melting ice, only to refreeze moments later with an even thicker layer of snow. The Millers were being buried under growing layers of ice and there was nothing she could do about it.

Even though it was warm where they were standing, she could feel cooler air currents drifting down to the river's edge. Ginger grew teary-eyed looking up at the grotesque ice prison. Then the tiny creature spoke.

"My name is Pan. Let me tell you what we know. I was placed in this dollhouse long ago by a fairy queen to guard the house and the magical items hidden inside. She told me of an evil creature who wanted those things. If the evil one got them, her dark powers would be unstoppable. Many people have owned this dollhouse since the queen put me here, and I have never been seen by any of them until I arrived here. I do not know why or how you and Becky were able to see me. Something that belongs in the dollhouse was removed or was not put back inside when it came here. That was not the only thing that went wrong."

Norm spoke. "That's right. For some time now, I've been sensing changes in the woods, smelling things that do not belong and seeing strange shadows in the woods. My nose has been glowing brighter than ever before. It is not my imagination; those trees are moving closer."

Ginger looked toward the darkening shadows near the edge of the stream. The woods did, in fact, appear even closer than before. Everything seemed even darker and more obscured in shadows.

"Aunt Fiona! She knows something about this. She was looking for the key. Pan, tell me about the key and Aunt Fiona. I think she is the one that did all this and took Becky. We have *got* to find Becky." Ginger was frightened but also determined.

"I'm not sure Aunt Fiona did this," Pan said.

Blaze agreed. "None of us saw her or Becky leave the house."

"Then who did this and how are we going to fix it? The day I found the dollhouse in that hidden room, I knew something was wrong, and things have gotten worse ever since."

"Things are *very* wrong, Ginger. Let's try to take a moment and see where we are, what we know, and what we don't know." Norm's calm voice steadied Ginger, giving her confidence of finding a solution. "Each of you, what do you remember from yesterday?"

Ginger, Rothschild and even Pan stared at one another. Norm said, "As I thought. You don't remember last night at all. And neither do I. The last thing I remember is watching the car as it pulled into the driveway, with Fiona. After that, nothing."

Blaze was next to respond. "I need to tell all of you something. I am not sure how, but I was inside one of the boxes in that hidden room. I was not in the dollhouse . . . at least I don't think I was. I remember flying out when the box was opened in Becky's room."

Ginger gasped, angrily. She felt her fur standing up on her back. "You were with the dollhouse? And then you were in Becky's room? Maybe you caused this!"

"No! I did not cause this. Norm, tell her. I came to help! This morning I was the first to see that something was wrong, and I came to alert everyone," Blaze said sternly. "Someone put me in the box to guard Pan. That much I am sure about."

Norm listened. He looked at Blaze, the giant dragonfly, and waited for Pan to speak.

Pan considered what had been said, "I believe him. I am not sure how you got here, Blaze, but the lady who put me in the house said that there would be others to help if something bad happened. I believe Blaze was sent to help."

"I agree," said Norm. "Blaze, I believe that you are here to help, and Ginger, I hope you will agree with me on this. Now is not the time for mistrust." He looked hopefully at Ginger, waiting for a reply.

Ginger considered how Blaze had gone with her into the frozen house and helped her find Pan. Whatever bad things that happened last night, she didn't think Blaze caused them. "I believe you, Blaze."

Rothschild had been listening without saying anything. The praying mantis had a way of blending into places and conversations that made people forget he was present. He said, "I know someone who can help us." He cleared his throat. "Someone who can help you find answers to the *real* problem."

"What is the *real* problem?" Norm demanded.

"We need to know what happened last night. Who did this? Who took Becky and Fiona? Where is the key? Assuming it is missing." Rothschild felt proud of his certainty.

Ginger jumped at the opportunity to find answers. "Yes, please go get him! We must find out what happened last night if we are going to find Becky."

Norm, Pan and Blaze stared at each other, considering if they should take Rothschild up on the offer. Norm agreed, reluctantly adding, "I believe we have been victims of a spell of some kind, and we are not going to be able to figure this out on our own."

The others slowly nodded, considering the possibility that their memories had been erased. Ginger confirmed her agreement by wagging her tail. It was decided.

"I will return soon, and we will get to the bottom of this." Rothschild's voice trailed off as he disappeared in the grass.

"I am going to fly around the house again and see if I can spot any clues. I will return soon." Blaze disappeared, leaving Norm, Ginger and Pan to wait by the stream.

Hours later, Rothschild returned carrying a small bag between his front legs. "Here we go," he said. "Just what we need if we are to remember. My connection told me this is something called a Seeing Eyeball Crystal Ball Sandwich Cookie."

"That is a mouthful," Blaze grimaced.

"It will help you remember," replied Rothschild, ignoring Blaze. "Eat it and, *presto*, you will be able to remember everything that happened in the past twenty-four hours. All the events of that day will reappear in your mind as clearly as if it was in front of you right now." He unfolded his front leg displaying three small wafers, each the size of a baby aspirin.

"Maybe we should test this out *on you* first, Rothschild," said Blaze.

Rothschild looked nervous. "Well, I was not the one who saw—"

Norm leaned over to smell the wafers. "Smells like bacon," he interrupted.

"Bacon? Let me smell it. That is one thing I can smell, it's bacon!" Yes, it smelled like delicious, nutritious irresistible bacon! Ginger bounced closer to inspect the tiny wafers, drooling.

"Wait a minute!" Blaze buzzed over attempting to knock the wafer out of Ginger's mouth. "We haven't discussed if—"

But it was too late. "Chomp . . . yum!"

Rothschild shrieked, "Watch out, you almost took off an appendage!"

As soon as Ginger swallowed the wafer, she started feeling the effects. Within a few seconds she felt disoriented and giddy, light on her feet, as if she could fly. She leaned her face into the breeze expecting the wind to lift her, and she attempted to flap her ears up and down. It felt like she was soaring, even though she was standing in the same spot.

The vision placed her over a field with a vantage point above the treeline. She could see a raging river that flowed into three waterfalls. The scene came into focus, bringing her closer, just above the river, and she could feel water splashing in her face. There were high cliffs surrounding the river. She heard a girl's voice whispering in her ear, telling her that she would travel to the waterfall.

"This is the place that you must go to. It is where you will find the key that will break the spell. You will travel to the waterfall to find the answers."

The voice faded and Ginger struggled to hear more, but all she could hear was the sound of the water. Then she was back in the farmhouse. It was warm, and she was sitting beside Becky. Aunt Fiona was there, too. She was in the past now. Ginger realized she was going to see what had happened last night.

She tried to leap into Becky's lap, but she could not move. She was firmly planted in position as an observer. Just as Rothschild told them, she could see what was happening, but she would not be able to change it. What was she going to see? Her tail wagged as she nervously anticipated the outcome.

Becky was setting up the dollhouse, arranging furniture as Fiona watched, and that's when it happened. The room became dark. Becky continued to play with the house as if she had not noticed that she was in a darkened room. Ginger tried to bark but no sound would come out of her mouth. A darker shadow grew from the far corner behind the dollhouse, hugging the wall and expanding to cover the ceiling. It was a winged, shadowy creature. At first it appeared without dimension, flowing and changing shape as it hugged the wall. Large wings opened and flapped loudly as they thudded against the ceiling. The creature had piercing, gray eyes, and Ginger saw the ghostly white, blurred image of its face. *Is that a face?* Ginger saw Becky gaze up at the phantom and smile. The girl appeared to be in a trance. She stood and walked closer, holding her hand out in a greeting.

Ginger barked a warning, but she knew it was no use; this was a vision of something that had already happened. She felt the fur on her back standing up as she battled her feelings of frustration, knowing she was unable to help Becky. The creature drifted to the floor, transforming into the shape of a young girl which then stood at the same height as Becky, with long blonde hair. Her gray eyes searched the room.

She approached Becky. "I want to give you something, Becky, something very important. Only you can have it. Let me show it to you."

Becky leaned over to see the object as the girl held out her hands which were still clasped. "It is so important that only *you* can look at it. I need you to take this pouch from me. Keep it closed. We need you to take it to the stream and drop it in. Hurry, we must do this *now*."

Fiona sat on the bed, watching but not speaking. Ginger looked around the room and saw herself, curled in the bed, asleep. She had been unaware that this creature had entered the house the night before. She felt her anger rising but realized it would do no good. All she could do was watch. She was about to find out what had happened to Becky who walked with the winged girl, together, outside to the stream. Becky seemed happy and relaxed with the strange being.

Ginger watched as Fiona followed Becky and the creature. When they arrived at the stream, she saw Norm sitting on his favorite rock, frozen, unmoving, with his nose glowing bright red. He appeared to be under the effects of the spell.

The creature spoke again. "Drop it in the stream. Do it now. This cannot stay near the dollhouse. You must drop it in the stream."

Becky attempted to give it to the winged girl, but she recoiled, refusing to look at it. "No, I cannot. Drop it in the water, do it now. Before she knows I am here. You must do it," she commanded, still looking away.

The statement startled Ginger. *Before who knows I am here?*

Becky opened the pouch to reveal it. The key was beautiful, clear like a diamond with tiny jewels on the loop where she was holding it. Becky walked to the water's edge, bent and released the key into the water. When she did this, the creature, her back still turned away from the key, raised a wing and the water began to flow forcefully downstream, blown by a violent wind storm. Ginger watched as the key was sucked into the torrent and disappeared.

Snow began to fall, covering the ground in white. The creature grew larger as it curled its wings around Becky and Fiona, wrapping them in a sheer cocoon. Quickly, she became covered in thick black feathers with glints of red fur on the wing tips. As she flapped her wings, gaining altitude, she dropped plumes of snow and sleet that cascaded to the ground in giant drifts. She flew back toward the house, disappearing inside it. Sensing the vision was fading, Ginger focused her mind as the creature re-emerged from the house. Ginger saw that she still had Becky and Fiona wrapped in the cocoon as she flew away.

Darkness. Ginger struggled to retrieve the final images from her vision, but they were gone. She saw Norm standing over her, his nose glowing. Blaze and Pan were huddled together, whispering. "Is she okay? Give her some air."

Once she was able to regain her strength, Ginger told them everything she had seen. They decided that there was no need for the others to eat Rothschild's Seeing Eyeball Crystal Ball Sandwich Cookie. They knew enough. This was the work of a magic spell, possibly an evil spell. Something immensely powerful entered the house last night and cast this spell and took Becky and Fiona.

The woods had grown darker in the short time that Ginger was in the trance. The house was hidden under growing layers of snow, locking Becky's frozen parents inside. By chance or as a direct result, Fiona's arrival to search for the key had made things go from bad to worse. Even though there was a lot they did not know, the group of animals had to enter the woods. The key had gone into the stream. It was the only lead they had in finding Becky.

CHAPTER 12

*May you have the hindsight to know where you've been,
the foresight to know where you are going, and the
insight to know when you have gone too far.*

—IRISH BLESSING

They decided to leave immediately. There was no time to delay. Blaze took charge. "A few things before we get started: Rothschild, you stay here!"

"No problem," said a relieved Rothschild. "I will be the lookout. You can count on me."

Pan gave Blaze a strange look but decided to leave it alone. He had enough to worry about without second-guessing Blaze. If Blaze felt Rothschild should stay behind, then he should stay put.

"When we enter the woods, everyone be quiet," Blaze said. "We don't want them to hear us coming. Not yet anyway. We stay together." He flew to Ginger's head, leaning over to whisper in her ear. "You're going to be just fine. You are safe with us. All right everyone, let's head out."

"Who or what do you think will be in the woods, Blaze?" Ginger asked, suddenly feeling unprepared.

Blaze ignored the question, but Norm helped. "He is assuming that something in those woods is waiting for us, and it is probably *not* friendly."

They started to walk in the direction of the trees where the stream entered near a small clearing. As they traveled to the edge of the meadow, the grass became taller and seemed to swallow them. Ginger pushed through the tall grass that clung to her fur, making it hard to walk. She felt blinded by the thick grass, and no air moved. She was panting heavily and her feet felt like they were tangled in vines. She could feel grass, gnats and goldenrod pollen collecting on her nose and tongue, adding to the sensation of suffocation. She stopped, panting and sneezing. Just over her shoulder she felt cool air sweeping between the thick blades of grass. She looked up and saw Blaze hovering, his wings beating as he flew close to her, blowing the grass away from her face.

"Having trouble, Ginger?"

Ginger was surprised that a small dragonfly could displace the tall grass and weeds. As the air circulated around her, a path opened, and she stepped free of the tangled mass of vines. With a vigorous shake, she fluffed her fur starting at her head and ears, wiggling to the tip of her tail. That felt so much better! "Thank you," she called out to Blaze.

He replied with a loud buzz. "Quiet!"

Norm whispered, "We'll be out of this tall grass any minute." To Ginger's right, Pan was hopping and trampling down grass like a steam roller. How was such a small guy doing that, she wondered? As she observed his aggressive trail blazing, she noticed that he seemed bigger. How could that be? Yes, he was bigger! The meadow grass only barely covered the top of his head now. "Pan, you're growing," she exclaimed.

Blaze returned to her with another warning buzz. "Stop here, everyone. The trail is going to get dangerous now."

With the next step the grass became thinner, and they could see the entrance to the woods where the meadow ended. A thick canopy of trees greeted them. Everything seemed quiet. No birds sang, no frogs croaked, no bugs hummed. It was morning, but darkness crowded around them as if it was nightfall. Without speaking, they stepped into the growing gloominess of the woods. Norm's nose illuminated the path, casting an orange light like the ember from a fire. Blaze flew higher and landed on a tall tree branch to look ahead, searching for the best path for them to follow. The stream flowed faster here than when it coursed through the meadow. Pan hopped over to the tree. With each hop, Norm and Ginger noticed that he was growing larger and larger. By the time he reached the base of the tree he was the size of a full-grown kangaroo. He looked up the tree to where Blaze had perched on the highest branch, but he did not wait for instructions. His eyes began to glow. They sparked bright blue light at first, then transformed into amber twinkling light with golden flecks. The glowing intensified as the golden specks swirled, and then lifted out of his eyes. The specks rained down onto the ground and covered the leaves at his feet.

At first, they bounced randomly like shimmering popcorn kernels that had escaped an overstuffed pot with a lid left ajar. Then they crawled methodically in all directions, illuminating a large circle around Pan. Ginger could see their tiny wings which were glowing as bright as miniature campfires. Some flew above the ground while others stayed along the now-brightened path leading deeper into the woods.

Blaze returned, and when he saw Pan's transformation he roared with laughter. "You are full of surprises. Not sure what you ate for breakfast, but I think there was fertilizer in it. Looks like you are going to come in handy."

Pan smiled and gave Norm and Ginger a nod.

They followed what Pan called his "glow-bugs" along the pathway into the woods that were becoming darker with each step they took. The glow-bugs were a welcome addition to the journey, casting light on a trail that had become treacherous with large roots and vines. Pan assured the group that the glow-bugs would lead them to the key. This made Ginger feel better as she considered the possibility that, if the glow-bugs could find the key, they would also find Becky.

Ginger glanced back toward what she thought might be the direction of home. Behind her the woods had closed in and there was no indication of the trail they had just been walking. She felt a growing unease with thoughts of being alone in the dark woods. Her directional compass was, even on her best days, unreliable. Now it was completely shut down with the farmhouse chimney no longer in view.

Norm cleared his throat as he tried to whisper, "Something smells bad up ahead. And another thing. I am seeing things."

"What do you mean?" asked Blaze.

"I keep seeing big dark shadows that move, I don't know how to explain it, but the woods are filled with them and they are moving with us. Does anyone else see them?"

Ginger started to tremble and shook her head. "Not me. I haven't seen anything."

Nor had any of the others. They stopped to consider if something was following them. Everyone looked in all directions as Blaze flew to a high tree limb to get a better view. He came down and asked Norm if he was seeing anything now. Norm looked around, then shook his head. "I think it's all clear. Let's keep going," the turtle said.

To encourage the group, Pan added, "At least our glow bugs are leading us the right way. They are my helpers in times like this in case I'm ever separated from the things that belonged in the dollhouse. I wasn't sure they would work, but it looks like they're doing a great job."

Hearing this, Norm felt better. "Let's keep moving on the lighted path. If I see the shadows get closer I will let you know."

They all agreed to continue along the lighted path that was leading them to the key, though Ginger went along reluctantly. She wasn't sure if following the path was the smartest move, and she was afraid of being left alone if the others pressed on without her.

As Norm, Ginger, Blaze and Pan entered the woods, Marin arrived at the farmhouse in her form as a raven. She landed by the stream unnoticed and watched them disappear into the darkness. She searched for Rothschild, and when she could not find him, flew to the snow-covered house, hoping to gain entry. The yard had disappeared under the avalanche of snow that continued to accumulate and cascade toward the green, lush meadow, creating a juxtaposed winter/summer. Even with the thick layer of ice that blanketed the house she could see the faint glow of the dollhouse. She stared into the window of Becky's room, mesmerized that she was this close to the dollhouse. She perched on the windowsill attempting to peck through the icy shield, but the barrier was impenetrable. Finally giving up, she flew back to the stream and waited. Soon Rothschild appeared from his hiding place.

"Where have you been?" she asked.

"I have been here the entire time," he answered, emerging cautiously from thick shrubbery.

"Tell me what you learned," she said with narrowed eyes.

"The Seeing Eyeball Crystal Ball Sandwich Cookie worked. Ginger told me of a shadowy winged girl who appeared in Becky's room and cast a spell on them. She tricked Becky into putting the key into this stream." He pointed to where the stream disappeared into the woods. "That is where the key flowed. They have gone after it in hopes it will lead to Becky."

"What else?" she prodded. "There must be more."

Ignoring her question, he asked, "Marin, who sent Blaze? And who caused this to happen?" He pointed to the growing fortress of snow and ice. "Will it continue to grow?"

Marin sighed. "Don't concern yourself with these matters. You are doing important work here, and you have done a great thing that will help your friends. But I must warn you, Blaze saw you with me and now he does not trust you. In fact, you may be in danger from him."

"I can take care of myself. No dragonfly can harm me. My jaws are powerful," he huffed, trying to sound unfazed.

Marin studied his face for signs of deceit. "All the same, remain here and stay hidden until I send for you."

"Is Becky okay?"

Marin's eyes widened. "We cannot see her now. She must be in 'The Hidden.'"

"What's The Hidden?" Rothschild flew to a closer branch, waiting for her answer.

"Do not concern yourself with these matters. Stay here. I will send for you soon." Rothschild watched as Marin flew over the trees, tracing the edges of the woods before soaring straight upward and disappearing.

Rothschild felt shaken and fearful about what he had just learned. Blaze had seen him with Marin. That was bad. He wanted to disobey Marin and go after his friends. Maybe he could help them, or at least explain to Blaze that he wasn't a spy. Surely his friends would understand. He needed to explain how Marin had convinced him that bad things were going to happen if he did not get Ginger to eat the Seeing Eyeball Crystal Ball Sandwich Cookie. Thinking about how guilty he looked made Rothschild shudder with remorse. Was it possible he had been tricked? Had he given Ginger something that might make her sick? Or worse? Did he *really* know that Marin could be trusted?

He thought about the day Marin had arrived. *How did she convince him to keep this a secret from his friends?* How did he know he was helping one of the good guys? *Could she be the winged girl that tricked Becky into putting the key in the stream? If so, was this a trick to injure my friends? Maybe she was the creature causing the horrible freeze!*

Rothschild felt panic as he thought about his encounter with Marin. The more he thought about it, the fuzzier it seemed. *Why did I help her? They could be walking into a trap. A trap I put them in.* He needed to go after his friends, but could he catch up with them? Could he find them? Of course he could, as he was an excellent tracker and could fly very fast. *Yes,* he thought. *I must explain myself. They need to know about Marin. Maybe Pan will know whether she is good or bad.* The decision was made.

Rothschild entered the woods flying close to the stream. The air grew cold and darkness surrounded him. *It's scary here,* he thought. *I hope they appreciate that I'm putting myself in danger coming in here. And completely alone.* He stopped to listen for sounds. Maybe another mantis or beetle? Perhaps a frog in the stream? It was silent. Only the sound of the stream. Not even the trees were moving. He made a chirping sound, hoping to get a response, but heard nothing and continued to fly.

He flew for what felt like hours, stopping several times to listen, hoping to hear them, but they had a big head start. He clutched the tiny bag that contained the two remaining cookies. Maybe they would be useful. He felt a growing unease that he had been tricked by Marin and had put his friends in danger. Was it possible she was following him now?

Deeper in the woods, Ginger's stomach started to grumble and growl. Norm was the first to ask if she was feeling hungry. "I could use some food myself. I wish we had brought something to eat." At that exact moment, the path widened, and they saw a beautiful patch of blueberry bushes beneath a grove of apple trees.

"Interesting timing," said Blaze. "Apples and blueberries growing in these woods? I don't think we should eat th—" But before he could finish, Norm was crunching an apple.

Ginger joined in. "I don't usually like apples," she said, "but desperate times call for becoming vegetarian."

Pan reached into his pouch and pulled out a tiny bag no larger than a pea pod. As he placed it onto the ground it grew into an enormous pile of Ginger's favorite brand of dog food.

"How did you do that?" Ginger barked happily.

"I couldn't let you go hungry. Or, worse, become a vegetarian."

After the meal Blaze asked Norm if there had been any more visions. Norm reported that he was seeing the shadows again, crowded around the trail ahead of them.

"What are the shadows doing?" Blaze asked as he stared into the woods.

"Nothing. The shadows are close to us, and back at the Millers' house. I am having visions of the house, and it's surrounded by shadows. The good news is that the trail behind us is empty."

"Well, that's something I guess," Blaze whispered as he watched Pan approach to join their conversation.

Pan spoke as quietly as he could. "I think this is only the beginning of your visions. I believe they will become more intense the closer we get to the key, so let me know when you have a vision. In the meantime, we won't tell Ginger. Things are about to start happening. Norm, I'm not sure why but the shadow things . . . I think they fear *you*."

Norm frowned at that.

"Blaze, why didn't you let Rothschild come with us? I am worried about that Seeing Eyeball Crystal Ball Sandwich Cookie thing he gave Ginger. Do you think it might have hurt her?"

Blaze started to answer but was interrupted by Pan who was

waving and clapping his hands. "Everyone! Attention please! Time to pull out our secret weapon. Blaze, we need you now in your *true* form! Are you ready, my friend?"

"I thought you'd never ask!" Blaze roared. With a sharp crackle his wings began to expand and unfold. His face took on a new shape and his nose extended to become more long and slender. His eyes grew large and his wings changed from gossamer to thick leather with red veining. He grew to almost seven feet tall. A long tail hugged the ground in sweeping back-and-forth motions that resembled a whip. His eyes glowed blood-red, and warm bursts of air streamed from his nostrils.

Norm and Ginger watched in awe of the transformation from small dragonfly to this powerful beast standing a few feet from them. Ginger wondered if it was really Blaze at all, and she expected him to come flying from behind this new creature that had appeared from nowhere.

"Blaze? Is that you?"

"You've got to be kidding," exclaimed a delighted Norm. "You are a Dragon? Oh, this is great. This gets even better. But, then, why am I here? Maybe I will just go back into my shell. Let me know when you need me."

"Oh no, Norm," begged Ginger. "Please don't. I need you! You can smell any danger! Please, Norm, stay out here with me."

"That's right," said Pan. "We all need you. Everyone has a part to play in our search, and everyone has their job to do."

Pan came closer and spoke directly to Norm. "Remember your talents, Norm, and your discussion with Blaze. You are the only one with that gift. What about your sense of smell and glowing nose?"

"What discussion with Blaze?" Ginger asked.

"Oh, nothing," said Norm. "You are right, Pan. We all have jobs to do and talents to offer."

Blaze's new appearance meant there was no pretending they could travel stealthily through the woods. He led the way, thundering loudly, tail swishing back and forth, knocking down bushes and sending sticks and debris flying into the air as he cut a wide path through the woods for his friends to follow. Ginger felt hard objects hitting her on the head and shouted for Blaze to please be more careful.

"That's not Blaze," Pan yelled. "The Nadonocks are here."

"What's a *Nadun-knock*?" Ginger called as another pellet bonked her on the nose.

"I call them tree folks. I did not think they would be any problem for us at all. I don't understand why they are attacking us." Pan bounced over to shield Ginger from injury as several more pellets soared over his head.

"Norm, what do you smell?" asked Blaze.

Norm replied, "Just the woods . . . but something else, too. Something far away. I'm not sure what it is."

Spiked grenades that looked like sweet gum pods rained down on their heads. Ginger watched as Blaze pulled in a deep breath, then held it.

Sharp sweet gum pods were landing everywhere, and they hurt! Ginger wailed, "He is a dragon, and dragons breathe fire. He is getting angry! Look at him!"

"Toast them, Blaze," Norm said. "Fire some hot coals at those *Nado* . . . what did you call them, Pan?"

"Nadonocks," Pan said. "Just call them tree folks! This is a mistake. They have no reason to be attacking us. If I could just talk with their leader!" Pan shouted, as he dodged the grenades.

Pan saw that Blaze was about to open fire, so he made one final attempt to get the attention of the Nadonock leader, yelling, "*Truce!* Let's call a truce before it is too late!" Looking at Blaze he pleaded, "Wait, Blaze! give them a chance."

Blaze looked puzzled as he shot a glance back at Pan. Pink smoke drifted from his nostrils, sputtering, then forcefully blasted toward the Nadonocks. A protective wall of pink smoke surrounded them. Norm lifted his nose to sniff. It smelled like they were in a most fragrant meadow. Roses, hyacinth, lavender, honeysuckle, tuberose, and gardenia scents filled the air. The spiked pellets that had been hitting them became flower petals. The ground was covered in beautiful splashes of purple, red, yellow, blue, and white flowers. As the smoke drifted up the tree trunks, green leaves were stripped bare and flowers grew, some with long vines draping toward the ground.

"Look at that," Ginger cried joyfully.

Some of the Nadonocks had been untouched by Blaze's fragrant smoke and were ready to relaunch. Pan leaped to the Nadonock leader before they had the opportunity to respond, snarling at them. "What is the meaning of this attack?"

Blaze inhaled, readying for a second blast from his nostrils. "The next blast will *not* be pink smoke. That was a warning. The next thing you feel will be fire and fury," he growled.

One of the giant trees bent down slowly, gazing at each of them. He looked at Norm. "I recognize you. I have watched you for a long time in your stream by that beautiful meadow. We did not know you were with them. We were warned that someone would be entering the woods that meant to do harm. We are the guardians of this entire stream and this section of forest."

"You have been misled," Blaze responded with a snarl. "We are looking for something that belongs to us. We are seeking a key. It fell into the stream by accident and we must get it."

The tree folk considered what Blaze told them. "So, you are the ones looking for it? There are others who are already here that have tried to take it, but they failed."

"Do you know where it is?" asked Pan. "My glow-bugs were following it, but they have disappeared." Everyone looked around to see if they could find the trail or the glow-bugs, but as Pan reported, the glow had faded.

"Describe the ones looking for the key," Blaze pressed, standing so close to the Nadonock that the tree felt his hot breath singeing his leaves.

"The one that came to us first appeared as a raven, but shape-shifted into a winged girl. She calls herself Marin. She spoke of another, someone more powerful than her, that seeks the key. Even with their powerful magic, they have been unable to get it. Also, Marin seeks the woman and the young girl."

"Fiona and Becky!" Ginger shouted.

"We have not seen Fiona or Becky. That key has brought change and disruption into these woods and we want it returned to its rightful place. If you promise that it is the only thing you want, we will help you. But before we do that, you have an immediate problem. The pellets that we launched at you, there are several stuck in the dog's fur. You must remove them quickly."

Everyone looked at Ginger and saw the sweet gum pellets embedded in her coat. Ginger felt an intense burning and whimpered, grabbing one with her teeth. Pan stopped her.

"Don't pull them out, they will do more damage."

One of the Nadonocks leaned over. "Break off some of my branches and cover the pellets with the sap. The pellets will fall out." As they worked to cover Ginger's fur with the sap, the sweet gum pellets fell to the ground.

"Make sure all the pellets are removed," the Nadonock said. "You do not want to leave any of them in your fur because that would be bad."

The Nadonocks that had been transformed into flowering trees by Blaze's smoke also gathered around.

"Tell us where to find the key," Blaze asked again. The trees pointed in the direction of a sloping valley partly obscured by a thick group of yew. Norm overheard the words "deep ravine and watch out for the waterfall." He turned his attention back to examining Ginger's fur for any remaining pellets. The tree's warning that leaving pellets in her fur would be bad had Norm worried.

In the excitement he had barely noticed that the tip of his nose was now burning bright red.

"Tone that thing down," Ginger laughed as Norm accidentally shone a bright light in her eyes.

"Sorry, I thought I saw one of those sweet gum bombs in your ear."

"That was amazing what Blaze did. I don't think he's from around here, do you, Norm?"

Norm agreed, then added, "I wonder what else he can do. And Pan. There is a lot we do not know about Pan."

"Norm, have you thought about why your nose is glowing so brightly?"

"Of course, I have, but no use worrying about it. I like my glowing nose."

"Me, too," Ginger agreed.

As they plopped down side by side, Norm felt lightheaded. He looked at Ginger and could see her mouth moving but he could not hear her words. An intense, disturbing vision flashed into his mind. In it they were standing by a roaring stream that overlooked a cliff. He stared down the edge of the steep overlook and realized it was a waterfall. There was a giant winged creature flying over him, and he felt that danger awaited them. In his trance he saw the key glistening in the stream beside the base of the waterfall. He knew this was where the key would be found. They would go there, and they would face the danger. Norm shuddered and closed his eyes. There was something else; he saw a girl standing by the stream, and she was speaking to him. Was this Becky? She was in shadow but, as she came closer, he could see that it was not Becky.

She spoke in an urgent tone: "They have found the key, but they cannot touch it. Ginger is sick, and you must help her. Ginger can get the key and break the spell that has trapped Pan." The girl looked away and her voice faded.

He felt himself being pulled out of the trance. He saw Ginger as she struggled to stand.

CHAPTER 13

*There is not a way into the woods for which
there is not also a way out of it.*

—IRISH PROVERB

As he entered the woods, Rothschild heard what sounded like dry leaves crunching behind him. As he always did with unknown sounds, Rothschild froze in place as he waited for the sound to become three dimensional. There it was. A girl walked towards him from the direction he had been traveling. She was the height of a young girl, maybe ten years old, but this was no human girl. As she came closer, he got a better look. The first thing he noticed were the fine wispy gray feathers that cascaded down her back. They opened slightly as she bounced through the leaves revealing long wings that draped to the ground. Her billowy silver hair blew across her face as she looked down to step over a large root blocking her path. She shook her head and brushed her hair back as she glided over the obstacle. He heard her humming as if she were preparing for a party. She stopped and looked directly at him, smiling. Her face had a carefree radiance, and her pale blue eyes looked gently at him like she had seen a long-lost friend. She stopped.

Impossible, he thought, *nobody ever sees me.* He remained still, believing that it was his imagination.

"I see you sitting there, silly mantis. Come out, I am here to help you."

Rothschild hesitated. What were the odds? Another mysterious creature finding him and recruiting him to do heaven knows what evil job? He stepped out and introduced himself.

"I am Rothschild, the praying mantis. I am a problem-solving mantis, but I suppose you know that already."

"My name is Tilly, and I know *all* about you, and your friends, the key and Marin. You have made a mistake helping her, but you were under the same kind of spell that is causing all these problems. Unfortunately, things are getting worse. Much worse."

"Why should I believe you? Marin told me she was here to help, but now I think she has hurt my friends. Maybe you are the same."

"You will see me again when I come to The Hidden where you and your friends will be sent. For now, you must find a way to trust me. Ginger will soon fall very ill, but not because of the cookie you gave. Take this and put it on her tongue and she will be healed. I have been sent to help Ginger break the spell and free the one who is trapped. You see, Pan is still trapped. It is Ginger who will break the spell. Tell the others."

He had so many questions he needed her to answer, but he struggled to find words. She smiled at Rothschild and looked deeply into his eyes. He felt like he was floating and tried to steady himself. She leaned over and, with her delicate hand, showed him the small vial. It was no larger than a pea and had a silvery thin thread attached. She placed it around his head. "Use this. It is the only magic that will save Ginger. If you do not put it on her tongue, she will die. You must trust me. You are almost there. Go to your friends and prepare yourself. I will not see you again until you are at The Hidden."

Rothschild felt woozy and disoriented as if waking from a long sleep. Tilly was gone, and he was near the stream, but in a new location.

He heard the faint sound of voices. He froze. When he did not see anything, he flew to a tall tree branch to listen. With his triangular head tilted towards the sound, he remained still. It sounded like Pan. He shouted with relief, "Thank goodness! I found them!"

"Ginger, can you stand?" He heard Pan say. "What's wrong?"

"My paw really hurts. I don't think I can walk." Ginger's voice was fading.

Norm called Blaze. "Something is wrong with Ginger."

"Try to stand up," the tree folk encouraged Ginger. Upon standing she yelped and flopped back down.

"What have you done to her?" Blaze angrily threatened.

The Nadonock leader, Griffin, replied, "This shouldn't be happening."

Rothschild flew as fast as he could toward the voices. He came to an abrupt midair stop that sent him crashing to the ground. He nearly fainted at the sight of Blaze as a giant dragon. He sprawled to the ground with his feet twisted in the air, leaves covering his head and wings.

Norm smelled him and interrupted the group. "Everyone, I smell him. Rothschild is here!"

Blaze roared angrily. "Keep him away. He is with the winged beast. Rothschild has led her to us. Can you smell him, Norm? Where is he hiding, Norm?" Blaze called. "I will end him here and now!" Blaze's wings were glowing red, and black smoke was billowing. The ground shook as he pounded his feet with rage.

Dazed, Rothschild attempted to kick away leaves that were stuck to his jagged sharp rear legs. He pulled frantically at his rear legs while fluttering his wings attempting to find safety.

"Wait," Ginger whispered. "Please, Blaze, give him a chance to explain."

Rothschild took the opportunity, although terrified about facing a dragon instead of a dragonfly. He stammered, "Please, please Blaze, everyone, I am here to help! I was fooled by the winged monster.

Her name is Marin and she *made* me believe! She tricked me. She said she was here to help but when she arrived just after you left—"

"She is here?" Blaze snorted, nostrils flaring. "She followed you?"

"No, I watched her fly away. She wanted to get inside the house, but for some reason she couldn't get near Becky's room. Another thing, the freeze is getting worse. I want to help. Please Ginger, I didn't mean to give you something that made you sick. I brought the Seeing Eyeball Crystal Ball Sandwich Cookies with me, and if you want me to, I will eat them."

"It's not your Eyeball Cookies that did this," Norm said, glaring at the tree folks gathered around.

"We had a little run-in, a misunderstanding with the tree people, and I was hurt." Ginger winced and limped toward Rothschild. "I just need a little time and I will be feeling fine. It is not your fault, Rothschild."

Rothschild pleaded his case. "On the way here, I met a winged girl, different from Marin. Her name is Tilly, and she warned me that Ginger is going to get very sick. She said that Ginger is the one that can break this spell and free the one who is trapped." Rothschild said, while warily watching Blaze.

"She is talking about Becky," Ginger said. "What did she say I need to do?" Ginger tried to stand but her legs buckled, and she collapsed, yelping.

Rothschild waved his legs and shouted, "No. It is not Becky . . . it is Pan!"

Ginger's eyes were closed, and her breathing was shallow. "What is happening to her?"

Pan looked at the others all gathered around. Each face stared helplessly at their friend. Pan bent over to lift her limp head and scoop her into his lap. He rocked her gently. "Wake up, Ginger. Becky needs you to wake up." Pan's mournful eyes dripped tears that clung to his downy coat as he was overcome with his sadness.

Norm joined in with determination. "Come on, Ginger, you must wake up now! I smell some delicious bacon cooking!"

Blaze felt steam and heat billowing from his nostrils as he scanned the trees for something to ignite. "We are not going to stand around and let her get worse!" He stomped his feet and paced toward Rothschild. "We need answers NOW!" He blew a violent stream of hot air at the mantis.

Rothschild tried to brace himself against the torrent but flopped helplessly against the Nadonock leader, Griffin's trunk. "Everyone, I didn't get a chance to finish telling you. Tilly gave me medicine for Ginger. She said it would make her well." He reached for the tiny vial wrapped around his head. "I have it right here." He grabbed at his head, but it was gone. "No, it can't be. . . I had it. It fell off somewhere. It must be in the leaves. Everyone, we must find it!"

Pan, who had grown considerably larger, remained still with his eyes fixed on Ginger, cradling her, gently rocking her and stroking her long ears. Blaze stared angrily at Rothschild. Griffin and the other Nadonocks looked helplessly at the mantis. Norm remained at Ginger's side, his nose glowing red, unaware that he was being lifted off the ground by an unseen force.

Rothschild pointed at Norm with his mouth open. Blaze raced over, attempted to grab Norm as he was being lifted higher. He looked at Griffin. "Grab him. Hold him down."

Griffin extended his largest branches over Norm, grabbing him in a leafy bear hug. "I have him," he shouted. He slowly lowered Norm to within a few feet of the ground near Blaze. "Make sure someone has him. I don't know what will happen when I let go."

Blaze looked through the branches at Norm. His nose was glowing as bright as a fiery hot furnace and Norm's gaze was fixed far in the distance. "Norm. Look at us, Norm. Are you okay?"

The turmoil they had not noticed that the air had grown cold. Snow started to fall, gently at first, and then as the wind blew faster, snowflakes swirled and dry leaves blew into their eyes. As the wind intensified, the snow felt like an assault, stinging them and making it hard to see. The world seemed to be disappearing into grayness. Griffin's branches were flailing now, and his leaves were being torn from his largest branches. He struggled to maintain his hold on Norm. Pan gripped Ginger even tighter as he sheltered her from the frigid onslaught. Rothschild took the opportunity, while he could still fly, to get to Ginger and Pan. They heard a thunderous boom, and Norm disappeared.

Norm felt the turbulent snow and wind blowing and tried to wiggle free and call to his friends, but he could neither speak nor move. When the frigid air retreated, the others were gone. Instead of being held in a tree, he found himself on a seashore covered in stones. Warm muggy air clung to the cool ocean producing a misty, disorienting veil that obscured his vision. He could taste the spray of ocean water on his face, and hear violent waves crashing around him. Saltwater burned his eyes as the water pooled around the bottom of his shell attempting to suck him into the sea. He responded by moving his legs in a swimming motion and preparing to dive into the water. But instead of being sucked into the sea, he stood firm, calming his mind as he waited and listened.

Norm's senses seemed heightened as his new reality came into focus. The red glow from his nose illuminated the rocky landscape and the tall stone cliffs that hugged the shoreline. The sun shone and the mist surrounding him swirled lazily in thin patches to reveal a bright blue sky. Waves rippled over rocks and the ocean breeze blew gently over him in a familiar embrace. He liked it here. The sun was bright, and the warmth felt familiar—like home. With a contented sigh he gazed at the azure horizon. He saw it approaching, black against the beautiful blue sky. He heard flapping wings of a large bird flying toward him. He looked up, squinting, as the bird lowered its head and flew between him and the sun. The bird's angle of flight cast a long shadow and draped the cliffs in darkness. As it flew closer and out of the path of the sun, he saw it clearly.

The creature was mostly black with sleek, oiled wings and a gray face with a predator's piercing green eyes. Its talons came down to grab Norm, but as it made the final lunge and saw the glow of the jeweled hook at the tip of Norm's nose, the predator bird reversed course and retreated towards the high cliffs, coming to rest on the highest peak. There Norm saw the partial ruins of a stone castle hugging the jagged cliffs. Once grand, the castle sat abandoned yet still beautiful. Norm could see the bird looking down at him from the remains of a terrace jutting over the cliff. He watched as another figure emerged from the castle walls and walked towards the bird. When the sunlight illuminated the terrace, he could see that it was a girl. She looked down at Norm and held out her hand. Norm felt the heat from his nose radiating as it became a laser blasting to her. The girl was wearing a delicate jeweled crown. At the center, the red stone glistened as his beacon connected with her. Without the sensation of moving, he found himself beside her in the beautiful, terraced garden. She smiled at him. "Hello, my dear friend."

His thoughts raced, trying to recall her and this place. It felt familiar yet obscured from his memory. The girl spoke again.

"We are all under the veil of an evil spell cast long ago. You don't remember me, do you, Norm?"

Norm searched for memories or images that might explain how or when he had known her.

"I am June. More than five hundred years ago, a young girl who had come from her home in Scotland to live here felt homesick. In her sadness, she was tricked by an evil witch. She knew her as Beira, but the witch has used many names. Some know her as the Queen of Winter. She tricked the girl to obtain the Enigma Stones and used them to obtain great power. Pan, who was once a fairy king, learned of the deceit and attempted to help the girl, but Beira cast the spell that transformed him into the cheetah-roo. The enigma stones that Beira seeks have been scattered, and even I do not know the location of them all. The spell has altered your memory as well as mine, and the memory of your friend, Blaze."

"Blaze was here, too?"

"We do not know how Pan got into the dollhouse, but we believe that it was for his safety, and that the dollhouse is near the place where many secrets are stored. Much has been hidden from my mind. Something has happened to cause Beira to return. I believe her return is why the crystals in your nose started to glow. The jewels in my crown have been glowing and I have been drawn back here, to this place. I do not know why. I am unable to go where you must go, but Tilly can go with you."

Norm looked at the large gray bird that had been by June's side. Her eyes were that of a predator, but in their depths lay a kindness that made him trust and like her. She stretched her wings and looked skyward as she transformed into the mirthful winged girl that Rothschild had encountered.

"Ginger is ill," said Tilly, "and she will die without the medicine that I gave to the mantis. We must go back. The medicine has been lost and the others do not trust him. They are very close to The Hidden. We believe that Ginger will release the one who will free Pan and break the spell that has altered our memories. The deep freeze that happened indicates that Beira is near. We must go." Tilly's voice was stern and commanding.

Norm's heart raced. *I must save my friend.* He looked at June. "Can you come with us?"

"I am unable to cross over to the woods where your friends are waiting. But you will see me again." June smiled, touching the red stone in her crown. Tilly touched Norm's nose and they disappeared.

CHAPTER 14

Deep within the winter forest among the snowdrift wide
You can find a magic place where all the fairies hide . . .

~AUTHOR UNKNOWN

Norm felt troubled as he and Tilly reappeared in the middle of a blizzard, At least four beings had promised that they were on the side of Norm and his friends. But he couldn't be certain that any of them was telling the truth, and he knew that at least one was not. *But who?* Was Tilly friend or foe? Was he bringing the enemy right into the heart of his friend's camp?

Norm knew he might be the smartest turtle on the planet, but he also knew that didn't actually mean a great deal, because many creatures were smarter than your average turtle, so, perhaps he could easily be tricked. Even if he was, at least they had Blaze. The dragon was on their side to protect the group. But was a dragon more powerful than a witch?

Norm looked around and saw that Blaze had ignited a fiery barrier around Ginger and Pan to protect them from the freezing temperatures and accumulating snow. Rothschild was clinging to

Griffin's highest branches, desperately looking for the tiny medicine vial that was most likely hidden under the snow drifts. The wind was howling through the Nadonocks' bare branches, now mostly stripped of leaves. When Blaze saw Norm and Tilly, he blew hot air and melted a path for them to come closer. Recognition flashed in Blaze's eyes when he saw Tilly, but he could not remember how he knew her. Tilly smiled warmly at him.

"Hello, my old friend. I wish you remembered all the adventures we have shared. In fact, I wish I remembered all of them."

Me, too, was Norm's fervent thought, but Blaze frowned. "You are the one Rothschild told us about. We have a problem. The medicine is lost, and Ginger has fallen into a coma. We cannot wake her."

Tilly looked at the snow-covered ground. Rothschild flew clumsily over to them, fighting the wind. "Thank heavens you are here. The medicine fell into this pile of snow, somewhere around here, but I cannot find it."

"First, let me see Ginger. We must hurry." Tilly urged them to follow her to where Blaze had created the warm shelter. Pan was huddled over Ginger like a protective parent, his face heavy with worry.

"She is not well." Pan stared at Tilly but there was no recognition in his eyes. Tilly placed her hands onto Ginger's chest. She frowned, "Oh dear. We must find the vial. It is all we have, and this medicine came from far away. There is no time to fetch more." Tilly spread her large wings and flew straight up. As she climbed, she changed into a large gray bird. They watched as she soared between the trees, flying high and then diving low to the ground, searching like a hawk for a field mouse. Her eyes glowed green, concentrating.

Blaze yelled, "Should I try to melt the snow with fire?" There was no answer from Tilly.

Twice Tilly dove into the snow with her talons outstretched, and both times came up without the vial. Everyone's gaze was locked on her as she flew in calculated circles that expanded outward with every flyover.

"There must be something we can do to help," said Rothschild. "I will fly from tree to tree to help with the search."

"The wind is too strong for you," Norm warned, but Rothschild had already flown away. Blaze blew a strong breath of hot air towards Ginger and then turned his attention to exhaling hot bursts of fire into the air. His efforts were creating a small protective ecosystem for the group, but near the perimeter snow was piling high, walling them off.

"Something is trying to keep us here," said Blaze as he continued to breathe hot air and smoke.

"It is Beira, the queen of winter. There are things I need to tell you," Norm said, shouting as loud as he could over the blustery snowstorm. Norm told them what happened when he disappeared, and all the things that June had told him about the evil spell and Beira.

"Beira is close," Norm said. "But something is keeping her away. I do not know what it is, but if she could get to us, I believe she would kill Ginger."

Norm shivered, not from the cold but from fear that whatever was keeping Beira from overcoming them might be slipping away. "We do not know how to fight her. I don't think June knows how to fight her," Norm said. "Blaze, do you remember anything about Beira? We have met her before, and we cannot remember? This is bad. Unbelievably bad. We are losing!" Norm felt his confidence waning. His best friend might be dying and none of them knew how to save her.

Blaze continued to breathe fiery warmth in all directions. "I need to help Tilly. I won't be long." He flapped his wings and blasted off the ground.

They had not seen him use his fire-breathing or acrobatic skills to the full until now. Once airborne, Blaze blasted a fury of hot air that melted the snow from a large area of the ground. Tilly flew over him continuing her methodical circular pattern as Rothschild bounced from tree to tree, hoping to see a glimmer of the vial. The wind was getting worse, and he was spending most of his time clinging to branches. *Why did I lose the vial? This is my fault.* Suddenly he saw a sparkling at the base of a tree. *Is that it?* Digging his sharp legs into the tree trunk, he edged his way to the ground and crawled carefully over leaves partly submerged in mud and snow. The pea-sized vial was wrapped around a hawthorn branch, floating in an icy puddle. Trying to contain his excitement, Rothschild made his way through the mire. After a few breaststroke paddles, he had the vial wrapped around his leg and made his way back to the tree. "I found it," he yelled. "I found it!"

Blaze and Tilly returned, and all gathered around Ginger. Tilly took the vial and gently placed the medicine into Ginger's mouth, helped by Pan lifting one of the little dog's floppy jowls. "That should do it. Well done, Rothschild." Rothschild beamed. *Redemption!*

Blaze watched the snow already accumulating around them after just a short break in his fire breathing. "How long before Ginger is back on her feet?"

"It should work quickly," said Tilly.

They gathered to talk about what they would do once Ginger got well. Tilly said, "I must guide you the short distance to The Hidden. That is where you will find the key, and Ginger will free the one who is trapped. Pan, we believe that trapped one is you, and that you are not a cheetah-roo at all. In the realm where we are going, you are a king."

"I don't know if I am a king, or what I am, but I am ready to meet my fate, find the truth, and most of all, I am ready to battle Beira." Pan's eyes narrowed as he flushed with anger.

"When we are close to The Hidden," said Tilly, "Norm's nose should glow very bright. But we must leave soon. The evil one is near, and her powers are strong."

"What about Marin?" Rothschild asked. "Is she helping the

queen of winter? Is there any chance she might be here to help us?"

"No, she is helping Beira. It is possible that Marin thinks she is doing good, but Beira can take many forms. She has tricked many over the centuries."

"Where will we find Fiona and Becky?" Ginger asked.

"I do not know. I am sorry. There are many things we cannot see or remember about the origin of the spells that Beira uses. We know that we must free the trapped one. I believe Marin will be waiting for us and we will have to battle with her very soon."

Blaze was concerned. "But how do you know that Pan is the trapped one, or the king? We believe that he was placed in the dollhouse to guard powerful magic that Beira wants. We need to get the key and find Becky."

"Look around us," said Norm. "How are we going to get through this deep snow?"

"We will fly," suggested Blaze.

"What if somebody falls off?" Norm asked. "What if Ginger falls off?"

Tilly reassured them. "That won't be necessary. We are at the entrance to The Hidden. Rothschild was holding on to it during the storm. This ancient hawthorn tree has been used as a portal in and out of the mortal world. It should carry us safely back to The Hidden where we will find the key, and Ginger can break the spell."

Pan approached the tree, rubbing his hands against the bark. "Yes, I know this tree. I remember. There is a doorway, and I have it, here in my pouch!"

Before Pan could finish his instructions, they heard *"Woof. Woof, woof, woof."* And there stood Ginger, once more looking healthy and strong, romping around wiggling her tail and panting joyfully. Everyone got lots of licks, even Rothschild. Tilly gave Ginger a big hug.

"I have watched you for a long time, ever since you were a puppy. There were so many times I wanted to meet you, but it was not allowed."

After the celebration Pan reached into his front pouch and took out a Victorian-style wardrobe mirror. "This is a special mirror from the dollhouse." He brushed off the snow from the base of the hawthorn tree to clear a spot to place it.

Smiling he said, "Wait for it."

The mirror started to grow. It got bigger and bigger and bigger until it stood thirty feet high. As the mirror grew, it attached to the trunk.

"What will it do?" asked Ginger.

"It will take us to the waterfall where the key is. At least, that is what I hope it will do."

"We will find Becky there!" Ginger shouted. She trotted toward the mirror, but Blaze stood in front of her, blocking her path. "Wait! We need a plan. Marin and most likely Beira, or winter witch or whatever she calls herself, will be waiting for us. What other weapons do we have to fight them? I will scorch them as soon as I see them if I see them. Tilly, what can you do?" Blaze asked.

Tilly frowned. "Much of my memory is gone so I am not sure what I can do. June gave me this stone and she told me that I would know what to do with it when the time came. I believe it can protect us against enemy magic."

Tilly held her hand open to reveal a green stone that looked like an emerald. "Norm also has one of the magical stones on the tip of his nose. It is most likely the reason that Marin is afraid of him. I don't know what other abilities Norm has, but June told me that Norm was with her centuries ago when they had their first encounter with Beira. Pan, is there anything else in your pouch?"

Pan put a hand in the pouch, but it came out empty. "The mirror has always been in my pouch. I did not risk bringing anything else from the dollhouse." He looked at Ginger with sadness. "Becky is not at the waterfall. She—"

Tilly cut him off. "We must go to the waterfall. Ginger, *you* must go to the waterfall. You are the one who will break this spell and free Pan. That must be our next move."

Ginger nodded in agreement. "I will do whatever I need to do to rescue Becky and get rid of this awful frozen world. My home is frozen, and Becky's parents are frozen. Let's go."

Griffin and the other tree folk said their goodbyes and wished the group safety and success. "We hope to see you again."

"You will know we have succeeded when the snow disappears," Blaze replied with a faint smile.

"We look forward to your victory and wish that we could help. We will guard the hawthorn for as long as we can."

CHAPTER 15

*The world is full of magic things, patiently waiting
for our senses to grow sharper.*

—WILLIAM BUTLER YEATS

The mirror cast a soft light in the snowy gloom. Ginger approached, looking for her reflection. She turned one ear toward it, listening to the gentle humming that vibrated in all directions. The others moved closer to see what might happen. The mirror's mahogany frame had grafted itself firmly into the hawthorn tree, making it impossible to tell where the mirror started and the tree trunk ended. The glass wasn't glass any more—it was a gel. They couldn't see through it, and it did not reflect what was in front of it. The surface moved and swirled, pulling in on itself like water being sucked into a drain.

"I don't know about this," Rothschild said. "Has this been tested with anyone before?"

"I never needed to use it," answered Pan. "But I trust what is in the dollhouse."

"How do we know we can trust the dollhouse?" asked Norm. "In fact, how do we know we can trust anything? What we know is that an evil spell is affecting us all. It has disrupted my memory, and Tilly's, and Blaze's. Who knows what else is untrustworthy?"

"We have to trust something," Ginger replied. "I trust all of you. But I agree, I am not sure about the dollhouse. I *never* liked the dollhouse. Not you, Pan, but something about the dollhouse scared me. Pan, are you *sure* everything in the dollhouse is *safe*?"

Pan bounced closer to the mirror and held out his hand. "I am not afraid of what is in the dollhouse."

"Can we get to The Hidden without entering through this mirror?" Blaze asked Tilly.

"No, I don't think we can reach The Hidden any other way," Tilly said.

Norm said, "In this storm it would be dangerous to follow the stream on foot. But it is possible the mirror could take us to a place where we don't want to go." He turned to Pan. "Step back, Pan. We don't want you to be sucked into it just yet."

Rothschild said, "I saw Marin trying to get to the dollhouse after you guys entered the woods. She couldn't. That may be a good thing, right?"

Everyone looked at Blaze, the biggest and most powerful of them all. "I say we go," he said. "I will go first, and blast anyone who looks hostile. Tilly, you enter last. Everyone agree?"

They nodded in agreement. "Okay, let's do it," said Norm.

Pan bounced on his hind legs. "I will make sure Ginger is safe, so I will be behind her. Everyone: stay close and try to hold on to the one in front of you."

Blaze approached the mirror and gently touched the surface. The humming and swirling stopped. He entered without hesitation and disappeared with Rothschild gripping his tail. Ginger, Norm and Pan clustered together, entering in a bundle with Tilly behind them, using her large wings as a basket to ensure that everyone entered safely. Griffin and the other Nadonocks watched and waited as the group disappeared. Once they were inside, the mirror's surface returned to glass. Golden embers crackled, launching sparks from its surface, then faded as the glass disappeared into the hawthorn's massive trunk, leaving behind no trace of the mirror.

The air on the other side of the mirror was noticeably fresher, and a modest breeze blew behind the seekers from the direction of the entrance, pushing them forward. A thick, cool mist engulfed them, making it difficult to see until their eyes adjusted to the low light. In their rush to enter the mirror, they had not stopped to consider how it would transport them into The Hidden, but now that they were inside it, the experience was at best disorienting and at worst, terrifying. Beneath them, a rapid current prevented them from controlling their steps or speed. They were being carried through the portal—not walking through it. A thick substance offered support that kept them from sinking, yet it was erratic, causing each of them to bob up and down. The quickly moving goo separated them, but once their eyes adjusted, they could see each other in the gray mist.

Norm's nose glowed brighter than ever, a beacon that Ginger found very comforting. Suddenly, the puppy could smell with an intensity she'd never experienced. *So many smells!* she thought. She smelled something very sweet. *Is this the way flowers smell?* she wondered. Next came food smells—meaty, spicy, salty, chocolaty, sugary, fruity. She sneezed as the senses overloaded her nose. She looked at Norm and he looked at her.

"I can smell!" Ginger shouted. Her tail was wagging wildly. "Anyone smell that?" she asked. She watched as the others tilted their noses up, attempting to sniff.

"Nope, I don't smell anything," remarked Rothschild, who was floating on top of the current, feet pointed upward, effortlessly drifting.

Perplexed, Norm watched Ginger as she continued to sniff. Her nose wiggled and her nostrils flared, causing saliva to drip from her flappy jowls, dropping a coating onto Rothschild. "Ick," he protested. "Turn off the drool, *pleeeeaaase!*"

With her tail still wagging with happiness, she shook her head, sending spit ricocheting everywhere. Pan, Tilly and Blaze laughed as they attempted to dodge it. Tilly shook her wings to clear them of the slippery ooze. "I see light ahead," she reported.

Norm pointed his glowing beacon towards the light. "Let's get ready. Who knows where we are going to be when we get out of here?"

"Or who is waiting for us." Blaze readied himself to incinerate any enemy that might be waiting for them.

The tunnel sloped downward, and they all landed into a grassy field.

The first sounds they heard were birds singing, frogs croaking and insects buzzing. It was the sound of the country on a hot summer day.

"This is good," Tilly said. "Feel how warm it is."

"Too warm," Blaze replied. He took the first steps from where they were standing, testing the ground under his feet. "We have enemies here. They have not given up. They will be preparing a welcome party that we won't like. At all."

Norm's nose glowed red hot. "I hear the river."

The others listened to the faraway sound of rushing water. Ginger walked over to Norm, listening. "It is getting louder. It is getting closer. I can smell...WATER!" Ginger ran in circles around her friends. "We need to get out of here," she barked.

There was no water in sight, but the sound of rushing water grew louder and became white noise drowning out the other meadow sounds. Everyone frantically looked for the river, but all they saw was grass and flowers of an ordinary meadow. Everything looked normal and tranquil, except for the rushing sound. Growing loud. Louder. Louder.

"Where is it coming from?" Blaze didn't wait for an answer. He flew upward and circled them. Tilly joined him, yelling back to their friends. "I see nothing but meadow in all directions."

Blaze and Tilly landed in a patch of tall grass. "There is no sign of water in any direction, only meadow. We should start walking," said Blaze, who turned to lead the group in the direction of a path that ran along the edge of the field.

The first wave crashed over them with the force of a tsunami and sent them blindly careening through the torrent of water. Ginger felt the tall grass buffeting her as she was forced along the meadow, dragging her paws, trying to get a foothold. She searched frantically for her friends and got a glimpse of Blaze behind her. He was attempting to get airborne when a second tidal wave rushed over his head. Ginger had less than a second to hold her breath before the rushing water grabbed her like a violent monster, pulling her down through the fast-moving current, making it impossible for her to get her footing.

Tilly jetted past her, caught in a rip current. Ginger saw the tip of Tilly's gray wing barely above the surface. There was no sign of Norm or Rothschild. Another onslaught of water roared over her head and Ginger went under, caught in the same rapid current that had Tilly. Panic built as Ginger struggled to find land. Her breathing was too fast, and she inhaled water.

Blaze resurfaced next to Ginger, his head barely above the water. He attempted to reach her, but the fast-moving current pulled Ginger downstream, who tumbled headfirst into a lake of icy water where she plunged deep, sinking until her front feet touched the bottom. Almost out of air, Ginger fought her way back to the surface, holding her breath.

At last she felt air on her nose. With the last of her strength she got her head above water and took a huge breath of air. The water was now calm. *Is the battle over? No, Beira was not going to give up that easily.*

Ginger floated to the water's edge, gasping, and clambered onto the shore. When she had the strength, she lifted her head to get her bearings. She looked back and realized that she had fallen over a huge waterfall.

A flash of red moved across the water. Ginger's ears perked up and her nose twitched as her friend came closer. Her tail wagged, spraying water in all directions. "Norm! Here I am! Swim over here." Norm skimmed the surface, his feet moving the water in long, effortless strides as he coasted onto land. Ginger greeted him enthusiastically.

"I am so happy to see you!" Laughing and crying, she licked his face.

"Ginger, are you okay? Have you seen the others?"

"I saw Blaze and Tilly way up there and they were in trouble. I have not seen Pan or Rothschild." Before Norm could answer, Ginger started calling for her friends, barking as loud as she could.

"I don't think they made it down here," Norm replied as his eyes scanned the high cliffs above them. "I was the first one over the waterfall. I saw you when you went over the edge, and I started swimming over to make sure you were okay."

"Oh no, look up there." Ginger saw Blaze lying near the top of the waterfall on a ledge. He appeared unconscious.

"What can we do?" she pleaded to Norm.

They saw a shadow moving overhead. It was Tilly.

"Where did she come from?" Norm asked as he squinted into the sunlight.

Tilly flew toward Blaze and landed on a large rock to steady herself against the rushing water. They watched as she leaned over and reached for something they could not see.

Blaze moved, then raised his head, looking at her. He appeared groggy, unaware of where he was or of his precarious position as he moved in clumsy, sweeping motions.

Norm and Ginger yelled in unison, "Watch out! You are on the edge!"

Blaze glanced down the edge of the waterfall as if seeing it for the first time. He struggled to get his footing, displacing rocks and sending them crashing down the waterfall. Tilly hovered above him at a safe distance until he was free of all the stones. With a final push he spread his wings and lifted himself out of the stream. Tilly spotted Norm and Ginger at the water's edge and flew down to them with Blaze by her side.

"Everyone okay?" Blaze asked, studying Norm. "Looks like your shell got damaged."

"It's nothing to worry about. Just a small ding. My nose is glowing as bright as ever, so I must be fine."

Tilly looked at Ginger and leaned down to inspect her coat, rubbing it gently. "I am fine," Ginger reassured, "but what about Pan and Rothschild?"

Tilly looked back up the cliff. "I flew up there looking for them but didn't find anything. What about down here? Norm, have you seen any signs of them?"

"I don't think they made it down here," Norm said, solemnly staring at the ground.

"They must be down here," Ginger said, sounding hopeful. "They must be here somewhere!"

Her nose started to wiggle. "I smell something . . . cotton candy." Looking at Norm, she said smiling, "That's Pan."

"Cotton candy?" Tilly chuckled.

"Yes!" Ginger said, trotting away, her nose stuck to the ground with barely a look back. "I smell cotton candy. This is great. I can track Pan. Follow me!"

Blaze said, "Okay, follow Ginger. Tilly can you fly over us? Maybe you will see Rothschild." Blaze's expression left little doubt that he thought Rothschild was dead.

"I bet Rothschild is with Pan. We will most likely find them together," Ginger said, barely stopping as she sniffed the ground. "Norm, I can smell *really* well."

"That's great news. I am happy for you, Ginger! But what's going on here?" Norm looked down. What had been dry land was dry no longer. Water lapped around his feet. It resembled gentle waves on the beach at low tide, but the water level was rising, pushing deeper into the meadow. He looked back at the waterfall. The volume of water flowing down the rocky cliff was increasing.

Before he could sound a warning, Blaze saw Pan's fluffy spotted fur peeking out from the tall grass, just steps from where Ginger was sniffing.

"You found him, Ginger!" They raced over to their friend who was curled into a ball, unmoving. Ginger snuggled her head close and licked Pan on his ears. His eyes fluttered, then opened. "What was that? What happened?"

"You are fine," said Blaze. "It's going to be fine. Give him a minute, everyone. He will be okay."

"Where is Rothschild?" Ginger asked Tilly who had rejoined them.

Hoping to soften the bad news, Blaze covered Ginger with his wing. "Ginger, we have to be realistic. Rothschild may not have survived."

"I'm sorry, Ginger," said Tilly. "I looked along the edges of the stream, but I cannot find him and there's another prob—"

"We cannot give up," Ginger interrupted. "Let's keep looking. I can probably smell him. Norm you can help."

Norm looked back at the waterfall. "We have a big problem, and I think Tilly saw it. Look up there! That water is going to flood this entire area. We could be swept who knows where at any minute. We have got to get away from this water. *Now!*"

There was no time to mourn the loss of their friend. Norm was right. The water was rising fast. Blaze took charge.

"Pan, can you stand? If not, get on my back and I'll fly us out of the valley."

"I am okay." Pan struggled to stand, shaking the water and mud from his coat.

CHAPTER 16

Always remember to forget the friends that proved untrue,
but never forget to remember those that have stuck by you.

—IRISH BLESSING

The winged girl appeared at the edge of the meadow, hovering beside the waterfall. Light sparkled around her from a tiny rainbow reflected from the waterfall's mist. She moved closer and the rainbow collapsed and turned downward to touch the water. Red, orange, yellow, green, blue, indigo and violet washed over the surface of the clear water, following her as she glided to meet the others. The entire lake glistened; it appeared static and no longer watery at all but rather like a mirror with a rainbow inside it. The lake was transformed as the girl traveled across it.

"You do not need to leave. You are safe here."

Her voice was one of authority and kindness. Norm was staring at her. Hesitant, unsure of his memory, he said, "I remember you. Don't I?"

"I have known you for a long time, Norm. I gave you the glowing stone and it has served you well and protected you from

Beira's evil magic." She looked into Pan's eyes. "I did not recognize you at all, my brother. I am so sorry that this has happened to you."

Pan looked puzzled. "What do you mean? Please tell me. Tell us everything."

"You have crossed into The Hidden. Mortals believe it only exists in their imagination. It is a place of fairies, monsters, ghosts, witches and more. But, as you can see, it is *very real*. This is the gateway to our world, and The Hidden is only the entrance. Blaze, Pan, Tilly, and Norm have lived here for thousands of years. I sent Norm to watch over you, Ginger. You have a rare gift and now that you have crossed into The Hidden, into our world, your powers are being realized. Already, you are different. You are transforming."

"Transforming? What powers? I don't feel like I have any superpowers," Ginger said, looking puzzled.

"You are a Sidhe Seer, and it is very rare to find one in *our* world. We never expected to find one in the mortal world."

"What does a . . . what did you call me? What do they do? Is it dangerous?"

"A Sidhe Seer is *very* powerful. First, unlike humans, you can see fairies. You saw Pan in the dollhouse, and you saw Tilly. But more than that, a Sidhe Seer can also cast spells . . . and break them. There are many things that you can do. Things you *will* do." She looked into Ginger's eyes.

"I am Xanderena, one of the few who remain from a royal and powerful line of fairies. Pan, you are my brother. Your name is Panvexa, but those closest to you call you Pan. You are the most powerful fairy in our realm, and before this happened you were supposed to take our father's place as king. Since you have been trapped in the dollhouse and transformed into this furry creature, our world has been slowly falling into chaos. Worse, Beira has become more powerful. We do not know how, but her evil magic has begun to cross over into the mortal world. It could be because you and the dollhouse were hidden there. We do not know how or why the dollhouse came to be in Fiona's possession, but she has a sister. Ginger, Did Fiona speak of her?"

"No," Ginger replied. "Who is her sister?"

"Her name is Catriona. We believe she is helping Beira. Maybe she is under Beira's spell, but we do not know for sure. Beira's magic has altered some of our memories—mine, Pan's, Tilly's, Norm's, Blaze's, my sister June's, and others. We have all been affected by Beira's spell. We hope when Ginger breaks the spell that will free Pan, then our memories will begin to return. There is something else you should know. Catriona is also Becky's aunt. Her bloodline runs through Becky, and Catriona is not a mortal."

Ginger gasped, trembling. "Not a mortal? Then what?"

Xanderena continued. "I believe that it was no accident that brought you to live with Becky. Something—or someone—brought you to her on that night, and whoever it was had a reason. June is my sister. She and Tilly have the gift of teleportation. Until recently, she was able to travel into the mortal world through what we call *the thin places,* and that is how we were able to see the dollhouse after Ginger discovered it. We were very fortunate that she was able to locate Marin, which led us to Fiona."

"*Thin places?*" said Ginger. "What are thin places?"

"Thin places are portals in the mortal world that allow for travel between there and our realm. You arrived here through a *thin place* that was created when Pan used the mirror to enter through the hawthorn tree. Ginger, the reason we are sure you are a Sidhe Seer is because you discovered the dollhouse. Beira's magic is very strong. The dollhouse is magical. It existed here, in our fairy realm. It belonged to our grandmother. Pan retreated into the dollhouse when Beira cast her spell on him. Even though it is an object filled with fairy magic, Pan was unable to see—or sense—Tilly's presence. Tilly could not find Pan, but you saw both. Do not underestimate the power that you have, Ginger. And I believe that when we free Pan we will also free ourselves from the spell Beira placed on us."

"Where is the key?" Ginger asked. "There is so much to do before we can rescue Becky. I need to find Becky!"

"We will take you to the key," Xanderena said. "We have been unable to get near it, but it is our hope that you can get it. If you are indeed a Sidhe Seer, you should be able to take it. Beira is the queen of deceit, trickery and confusion. She has begun an attack on the mortal world and on *our* world. There are only a few of us left strong enough to hold back her powers here in The Hidden. And, Pan, there is something else you need to know: You have been trapped in the dollhouse for the past five hundred years by a spell that Beira cast in retaliation for something you did with her magical stones. Now we have a chance to break that spell and free you, but when you are free it will start a war between us and her evil army of fairies and shapeshifters. We must be ready."

Pan looked stunned and then agitated. "I thought I was in the dollhouse to guard it and the magic it contains. Now I discover I was changed from a warrior king into this . . . this . . . this candy-scented cotton ball with giant kangaroo legs. I am going to kill her!"

"You will get your chance, Pan," June said. "But first we must see if Ginger is indeed a Sidhe Seer. If she is, she will be able to take the key. We know where it is. We must hurry. Already Beira's magic is affecting The Hidden. Look around us."

They looked around. Where flowers had been blooming moments ago, there was now a thin covering of frost. Blaze blew a hot puff of his breath into the cold air, melting the icy glaze. The cliffs above them were now covered in heavy wet snow.

June said, "Ginger, are you ready?"

"Look, I don't know whether I'm a Sidhe Seer or not. If I can get the key, I will. And I hope Pan is freed and everything goes well for all of you against Beira, because Beira doesn't sound like a nice person to me. In fact, I think she's probably horrible. But you need to know that all I have in my mind is Becky and her family and that lovely farmhouse that's now frozen solid. I don't wish harm to anyone here, but whatever I do, I'll be doing it for Becky."

"We understand," said Xanderena. "Now let's get on with the job. Follow me."

She led them back across the rainbow-colored passage to the base of the waterfall. Rushing water pounded the stream's surface, churning waves that splashed over the temporary bridge that Xanderena's magic had created. She said, "This is as close as we can get to the waterfall. The key is in there."

"If Ginger goes into the waterfall, she'll drown.," Norm cautioned. "I'm not letting her go in there by herself. Forget it."

Xanderena said, "She is a Sidhe Seer. She will not be injured."

But Blaze said, "You mean you *think* she's a Sidhe Seer. Probably. If luck is on our side. I agree with Norm. She is not going in there. We must find a safer way."

"She has to. We've tried to stop the waterfall and get the key, but we couldn't do it. It has been getting stronger. Ginger will be safe."

Pan said, "They are right. We cannot risk Ginger going in there. Not to free me. I am not comfortable with this. It is too big a test. What if you are wrong and she is not a Sidhe Seer?"

But Ginger was having none of it. "Will you all please stop talking about me as if I wasn't here? Becky needs me to get that key and I'm going to get it or die trying." And she walked past Blaze with a reassuring smile.

As Ginger approached the roaring waterfall, Norm said, "I'm going with her. Water may not be a dog's natural element, but it is mine." As he glided past Ginger, his nose blasted red light into the water and sent silver sparks flying into the air.

Ginger trotted faster to join him. "I see it," she shouted. "I see the key!"

"Oh, thank all the Powers of Good," said Pan. "She *is* a Sidhe Seer."

The water began to thicken into a clear goo. Blaze looked amazed. "Look at her. She is glowing."

And it was true; Ginger's coat glistened with a silver aura.

The waterfall slowed and became crystalline, and small pellets danced across the bridge. Pan reached down to pick up a handful, grasping what first appeared to be ice pellets. As he slowly opened his hands he held his arm out to show his friends the glistening stones. "Diamonds."

Norm and Ginger disappeared into the crystal waterfall. The others watched as the red glow from Norm's nose bounced off the falling diamonds, lighting the sky a deep crimson.

"It's beautiful." Xanderena gasped.

Norm's nose targeted the key with a ruby red laser beam. Ginger looked behind them at their friends on the other side and called out to them. "We are fine!" Looking back at Norm she whispered, "I don't think they can hear us."

"I do not think they can hear or see us." Norm replied as he stared at the key.

"Who is making this happen?" asked Ginger. "You or me?"

"I think this is you, Ginger. I felt a push into the waterfall, and I think you were the one pushing me."

Ginger walked to the key. The smells of cotton candy and bacon were strong. "Do you smell that?" A vision of a dragon appeared. More images followed, slowly at first, then flooding her mind in rapid fire, making her disoriented. Everything was spinning past her, creating a blur of images and colors. When the spinning stopped, everything became very clear. Ginger knew what she must do with the key, where they would go and what would happen. The sensory overload knocked her down and she sprawled against the back wall on the cliff floor. Her eyes fluttered open and she saw Norm staring at her, his nose touching her nose.

"That is too bright, Norm!" Ginger said. "Turn it down a notch."

"Sorry. What happened?"

"I saw the spell being broken. I know what comes next. Come on. Follow me!" Ginger picked up the key in her mouth without hesitation.

"Lead the way," said Norm. "I am behind you." They emerged from the diamonds with the key safely in Ginger's mouth. She placed it on the ground in front of her friends.

"I know what we must do," she said. "I had a vision. We must act quickly! The creature that came to my house the night of the deep freeze, she came to help us get this key here. She is the one who wanted Becky to drop the key into the stream. Because of her magic, that stream transported the key here. Only here in The Hidden can the spell be broken. This is where I was supposed to go. In my vision I saw Beira chasing the creature that got Becky to put the key into the stream. The creature took Becky and Fiona someplace safe, but I could feel her fear, as she knew that Beira was close. It was Beira who arrived later that night and cast the spell that froze everything. That spell is getting worse. Beira is near, and she is looking for someone else. She knows we are going to free Pan. Tilly, the stone that you are holding, the green stone: Place it on the top of the key."

Tilly produced the emerald stone that June had given her and put it into the round open loop on the key's handle. It stuck in place as if it had always been there. A golden crown appeared hovering above Pan.

"Pan, take your crown and place it over the key."

Pan took the crown as Ginger asked. The crown broke open and twisted around the key in a snake-like spiral, squeezing together until the crown and key were one. Sparks flew as metal and glittering stones were reshaped into a long scepter. Bright red and blue lights glowed from the sapphire and ruby that illuminated the tip of Norm's nose. The lights attached to the scepter like a magnet and pulled it upright. From inside Pan's pouch a small object flew towards the scepter.

"Ouch," yelped Pan. "What was that doing in there?" Everyone stared, unmoving, as they watched the small object attach to the top of the scepter. Xanderena recognized the object.

"Pan, it is our father's royal ring. It had been lost!"

Ginger walked to Pan and placed her front paws firmly on his chest. "All you need to do is touch the scepter and the spell will be broken. But you must hurry. I have seen a vision of Beira. She is near. Something is preventing her from entering The Hidden, but others are coming to join her."

Pan walked to the scepter, which burned with red and blue flames. The tiny ring hovered over the top of the scepter. It dazzled in green, purple and orange brilliance from the golden band that was covered with emeralds, rubies and sapphires. In the center of the ring, a large black stone glowed, siphoning the colors from the other stones, becoming a miniature celestial black hole.

Ginger said, "The ring will slip onto your finger when you touch the scepter. In my vision I saw you restored to your true form as king."

Tears filled Pan's eyes when he touched the scepter. The transformation began. A flurry of sparks and fire rained down over the group that huddled around him. Blaze moved closer, spreading his wings to block falling embers. The flames spun like a tornado around Pan, then changed into a swirling snowstorm. A white light grew so bright that everyone closed their eyes.

Only Ginger's eyes remained open.

"It has happened. The spell is broken," she yelled over the loud wind. The kangaroo legs had disappeared, and Pan gripped the scepter. Pan's blue eyes blinked as he tried to focus, and the last remnants of the dying windstorm blew his long hair across his face. Nothing remained of the furry cheetah-roo..

The wind stopped. Pan opened his eyes and inhaled a deep breath as he took his first steps. In every way, he looked powerful, confident, and ready to lead. He stood taller than both Xanderena and June. His face appeared strong with high ruddy cheekbones that accented his pale features. His thick white-blonde hair cascaded to his shoulders in ringlets that looked disheveled, hinting at his mercurial origins.

Surprised, Blaze said, "Pan, you have no wings!"

Pan glanced back casually with a bemused smile. "Not all fairies have wings, Blaze! This proves that the memory spell is still affecting us. We have known each other for a thousand years my friend, yet you did not remember this about me. How many Aos Si remain in this part of The Hidden?"

June looked sadly down at the ground. "We are scattered. We do not know how many remain. There are maybe twenty here, in this place."

CHAPTER 17

A kind word never broke anyone's mouth.

—IRISH PROVERB

I t was early morning when Marin arrived at Catriona's seaside cottage. The setting sun cast an orange glow on the surface of the ocean. Catriona was sitting in her garden, bundled in a thick shawl to keep warm as she waited for Marin's return. The weather had deteriorated, the temperature dropping into the forties, with the wind whipping from the north. The ocean mist blew over the cliff walls, spraying dampness on Marin's face and hair. She considered retreating to indoors, but felt compelled to stay where she could get the best views.

"I have been concerned about you," Catriona said. "I expected you back before now. Please tell me you have good news."

"When I arrived at the farmhouse, Becky and Fiona had vanished, and the key was missing," Marin said. "I was able to get the mantis to help us. The key has been removed from the dollhouse by Becky and is at the waterfall, but as you know, I cannot get near it. I tried to gain access to the dollhouse, but I couldn't. Pan is with them."

Catriona exhaled with force. "Did the key cross into The Hidden?"

"Yes. All of them are there. But I have been unable to cross. Something is preventing me from getting back into The Hidden."

"I have read the diary looking for clues. I am convinced that Fiona has the section of diary that came from Beira. She deceived our family five hundred years ago. But if I am wrong and it is the diary—*my diary*—that was penned to deceive, then I will be the one who brings all this darkness back into full power." Catriona's voice trailed off as she considered the possibility that she had been wrong.

"There is something else," Marin continued. "Something else is searching for the key and I fear it may have captured Becky and Fiona. The house is an icy tomb covered in an avalanche of snow . . . and it grows."

Hearing this, Catriona opened the diary and quickly flipped through the pages. "I have read about this happening before. Where was it written?" She turned the pages rapidly. "Yes, here it is." Her eyes scanned the pages searching for clarity.

She read, "Over a thousand years ago, a powerful clan of fairies called the Aos Si crossed into the mortal world. They helped the humans that lived here, in this part of Ireland as well as parts of Scotland, teaching them blacksmithing, weapon making and skills that would defend humans against evil spirits that had invaded this region. Many of the lochs and the sea between County Antrim and Scotland were inhabited by evil beings that wished to harm mortals. Our family befriended the royal clan of Aos Si until an evil witch named Beira waged a battle with our family and the Aos Si."

Catriona turned the page but noticed something that she had missed before. "No, it can't be." She frowned, flipping the pages forward then turning back. Her hand held the book open as she studied the binding. "There are pages missing. There are *a lot* of pages missing. They have been torn. I was told by my mother that our family has a secret. She would never tell me what it was. We need Fiona's copy of the diary. Can you get it from her house? Now that she is no longer there, maybe you can gain access."

"I was unable to enter when Fiona was there," Marin said. "Maybe now I can get inside." Marin looked out at the darkening horizon.

"Go, get into the house and find it. Bring everything that is there. The diary, the necklace, and the box. I am going to The Hidden."

Catriona pulled the black stone from her pocket and admired it.

Marin's eyes narrowed. "How will you get into The Hidden? I have been unable to enter."

"I believe that this stone will allow me safe passage," Catriona whispered. "I do not know why, but I feel that I am supposed to go. I am having visions of a young fairy king. He is speaking to me, but I cannot hear what he is saying. There are other fairies there, and a dragon. I must go. You will take me to the thin place in the woods, near the entrance. Leave me there. If my plan works, you will be able to enter The Hidden when you return from Scotland. But fly over the farmhouse first. I want to see it."

Catriona raised her arms so that Marin could grasp her shoulders with her giant talons, and Marin rose into the air with her precious burden. They flew over the seaside cottage, and Catriona was overcome with melancholy that she would not see her home again. Marin turned sharply, gaining altitude to fly along the edge of the cliff walls that hugged the shoreline. Catriona glanced back at her home, scanning the darkness for a last glimpse of her garden. With another sharp turn, Marin glided over the ocean before they disappeared together in a shower of magical silver sparkles.

When they arrived in Vermont, Catriona gasped to see the mountain of snow and ice that had engulfed the farmhouse. The entire state of Vermont had fallen into the clutches of a violent blizzard. No cars moved, and power seemed to be out all over the region. Marin landed beside the house in which only the upper story window was visible. A tiny light flickered through the icy glass.

"The dollhouse," said Catriona. "Look. There inside, the light glows! Take me up there."

Marin obeyed, scooping her up in her talons, and flew to the snow bank that hugged the windowsill. Catriona struggled to gain her footing, bracing herself against the glass. She touched the window. "It is warm," Catriona said, with wonder. "It is holding back the evil magic of Beira. Even with Pan no longer inside." She thought about all that had transpired. "What is the secret my mother would never tell me?" Touching the glass again to feel the warmth. "There is something wrong. Something I have missed."

Catriona held her arms out, signaling to Marin that it was time to leave. Marin glided low over the stream, allowing her a final look at the farmhouse, as she flew toward the tree line. Most of the leaves had been stripped by the snowy onslaught of Beira's magic. Catriona wondered about the Nadonocks that lived there near the thin place. When she was younger, her mother had told her about the creatures that guarded the entrance to The Hidden. The Nadonocks were her favorites. They had once dwelled near her seaside home, before that entrance to The Hidden had vanished.

She signaled for Marin to land. "This is the place."

Marin descended, landing gently and placing Catriona in a sheltered spot under the trees. The air was unbearably cold, and she wrapped her thick shawl tightly around her face. "You must leave," Catriona prompted.

Marin stared at her, unsure. "I can fly just over there and make sure you get through."

"No. I must go alone. It will be fine." She watched as Marin reluctantly flew over the trees headed to Fiona's home in Scotland. Catriona did not believe that Marin would be successful in getting the diary or the other items. There was something powerful keeping her from reaching them. More important, she wanted to make the journey into The Hidden without Marin.

Catriona looked around for the Nadonocks, and considered calling out to them. The woods were cold and strangely silent. As she grasped the black stone firmly in her hands, she petitioned, "I hope you still have some magic in you."

She held her arms outstretched as she walked to the giant hawthorn tree where the others had passed through. As she got closer, she felt the stone getting warm. She opened her fingers slightly to peek at the black light glowing in her palms. "Good. This *will* work." She touched the bark of the giant hawthorn. "Hello, fairy tree.".

The bark melted away as it pulled her into the mysterious opening. The imperceptible veil opened. The air felt warm and humid. She tried to walk but her feet would not contact the ground. She grasped the stone secure knowing that, if she dropped it, she could be trapped. She felt suffocated by the fear of being stuck there, in between The Hidden and the mortal world. She had not traveled into The Hidden since she was a young girl. Panic threatened as she tried to control her breathing. She brought her hands together, pulling them close to her chest to occupy less space as she floated through the thick white mist. The warm stone made her feel calm. She focused on the comforting glow in her hands as familiar images took shape in her mind.

Memories surfaced of her time spent in The Hidden with her mother. The memories felt distant and fuzzy. She tried to focus, to remember, but the images faded. She felt a cool breeze on her face as she emerged. Her legs felt heavy. The bright light was disorienting. She sat, hoping the feeling would quickly pass. Concerned about what might be waiting for her, she struggled to her feet and took several deep breaths to clear her head. The air felt fresh.

"This feels like my seaside home. It feels like I am home."

In the distance she heard voices and saw flashes of colorful light. She made her way through the meadow toward the rocky cliff just as the spell was broken and Pan made his transition. The waterfall remained static. She stood leaning over the edge to get a better view of what was happening below. She recognized Xanderena and June, but who was the handsome man with them? She saw the dragon. Her eyes narrowed, and she readied herself for a possible attack.

"Blaze. You are the unpredictable one, so Marin tells me."

A nearby voice startled her. "Excuse me. Could you please help me?"

Catriona looked around but did not see anyone. "Hello, where are you? I hear you but where are you, invisible fairy creature? Show yourself."

"I am neither invisible nor a fairy creature. I am however, stuck under a rock. Look. My wing is just below your foot."

Catriona looked down and saw a glint of green poking from beneath the rocks. "You are an insect?" She bent down and picked up the stone.

"That feels so much better. My sincere thanks to you. Let me introduce myself. My name is Rothschild and I am a praying mantis, a problem-solving praying mantis, I fix—"

"My goodness, I know who you are." Catriona laughed. "I cannot believe you made it here, to The Hidden. Marin said you were resourceful, but I had no idea how resourceful."

Climbing onto a large stone to get a better view, Rothschild asked, "Marin? How do you know Marin?"

"I sent Marin, and I gave her the Seeing Eyeball Crystal Ball Sandwich Cookie that you gave to Ginger. So, thank you. You have been most helpful."

Rothschild backed up, trying to find an escape. "Well, I will be heading back now. See you later. Thank you again."

"Wait a minute. Why aren't you with them, down there?"

"I got separated during the tidal wave. I guess they think I am d—" He stopped what he was saying. *This person could be extremely dangerous*, he thought.

Sensing his fear, Catriona leaned down. "You think I am here to hurt them? Hurt you? Don't be silly. I am here to *help* them. Help Pan, and Ginger. If I can."

"That's great, but if you don't mind, I will just stay here."

Catriona scooped him up. "Don't be silly. Come with me. Maybe if that hothead Blaze sees me with you he will hold off any foolish attacks. He has a hair-trigger, you know. Marin tells me he blasts first and asks questions later."

Catriona pulled the black stone from her pocket and held it in her left hand. She closed her eyes. Rothschild, terrified, tried to wiggle free, but she was holding him securely. She closed her eyes and spoke to the stone. "Take me to them."

They were transported to the place where the others had gathered, appearing in a misty puff of air.

"Catriona!" Xanderena cried out.

June stepped between Catriona and Pan. "She is with Beira."

"No, that is not true," Catriona pleaded. "You are mistaken."

Rothschild fluttered out of her hand and flew to Blaze. Pan, Ginger, Norm and Tilly watched as their friend flew clumsily through the air. "Rothschild, you are alive!" Blaze greeted his friend with puffs of white smoke before turning to face Catriona. "She had Rothschild. What did you do to him? I am going to torch her."

"Wait!" Ginger raced over to Blaze. "No, she is not with Beira. I saw it in my vision. She is one of you. She is Aos Si."

Everyone stared at Catriona.

"No, that cannot be true!" Catriona protested. "I am not one of you. I was born in County Antrim, Ireland. I am mortal, not Aos Si." She pulled the diary from her shawl. "See, look." She flipped the pages. "This is where it is written about my birth. I was born with the gift of sight, just like my mother, to communicate with the Aos Si, but I am not one of you. That is not possible. I have a beautiful seaside cottage in Ireland. That is where I belong."

"Nevertheless, I saw it in my vision," said Ginger. "Soon you will see it, too. All of you will see it."

June paced, impatiently, as she listened to the discussion. "I do not trust her. Xanderena saw in a vision that the betrayer is in the mortal world, in County Antrim. That is where all this started, where the old castle stood a thousand years ago, when we trusted mortals. That is Catriona's home. She has fairy magic in her blood, and she has most likely allowed Beira to enter The Hidden."

"That is not what I saw in my vision," Ginger countered.

"We must listen to Ginger," Norm said. "I do not believe that Catriona is our enemy. Who else agrees with me? We have seen with our own eyes that Ginger is a Sidhe Seer. Her visions can be trusted."

"We may not know who our enemies are," Pan said. "We will deal with Beira, but I have made a promise to help Ginger find Becky. If that means facing Beira, that is what we will do. For now, we are going to trust Catriona. Even though the spell that trapped me has been broken, we cannot be sure that our memories are intact. For that reason, we will rely on Ginger to guide us at least until we are sure that Beira's spell on all of us has been broken."

Everyone nodded in agreement, and Rothschild took the opportunity to speak. "I for one am very happy that Catriona showed up to free me from the boulder that had trapped me. Without her, I would have surely died. Thank you, Catriona, for not leaving me there."

Catriona, who had been fearing for her own life moments ago, flashed a warm smile at her new friend. "I was most happy to help you. I want to help all of you, including my great niece who I have never met. I sent Marin to Scotland, to Fiona's, hoping that she could get inside and bring the other copy of the diary. I wanted to prove to Fiona that she has a diary that was penned with Beira's evil magic. Deceived by what was written in that diary, I fear that she is helping Beira and does not know it. Marin had attempted to get inside Fiona's castle, but she told me that something prevented her. I instructed that she return to the hawthorn tree and wait for me. If she has returned with the diary and other things, they can only help us."

"No, you are wrong. You are very wrong. You have no idea how close you have been to Beira your entire life." Ginger's words came out in a prophetic rush. Her eyes were unblinking, glowing as her Sidhe Seer powers continued to strengthen. "*Marin is with Beira.* She has always been with Beira, and she was sent to watch over you and to prevent you from ever knowing who and what you are. She kept you there in County Antrim, away from here and away from the dollhouse. Away from your family. Away from the truth. Marin is a great threat to all of us."

Catriona's breath hung in her throat as she processed what Ginger had said. "I have trusted Marin for most of my life. She is my best friend." She fell to her knees, sobbing. "All the times I thought about visiting Fiona or other family members, it was always Marin who convinced me to stay away. So many lies."

Xanderena, June, and Tilly flew over, forming a protective circle around Catriona, hugging her and wiping the tears from her face. Their wings drooped, and they wept as they shared in her grief and anger. Catriona hugged them in return until her sobs quieted. They remained huddled around her, their wings now fluttering wildly, sounding like a small engine. A yellow glow shone in the center.

Ginger spoke up. "I told you. Everyone would see that Catriona is one of you. Look."

Catriona stood up and walked toward Pan and the others. Transformed, she appeared as a young girl with long auburn hair and sea-green eyes. Her skin was fair, her face made with delicate features, but she was taller than both June or Tilly, and without wings. "How did this happen?" Catriona asked, as she twirled in a circle.

Ginger's eyes were still glowing, as if in a trance. "This is your true form, Catriona. You are Aos Si, but you are also human. I believe truth has freed you from the spell. My vision did not reveal how you came to be this way, but I trust that in time, you will learn."

"Thank you, Ginger. I am glad that I am here with all of you, but it feels like a dream."

Catriona gave her copy of the diary to Pan. "I think we should keep this here where it will be safe."

Pan took the diary. "Thank you, Catriona." Their eyes locked in a familiar gaze. When his hand touched her fingers, she felt a warm flush on her face, making her cheeks glow red.

"No more argument about Catriona," Pan commanded. "My powers are back. My memory is returning, and I am ready to lead those that will come with me to rescue Becky. Is there anyone here who doubts me? Anyone that wants to bail out? If anyone wants to leave, now is your chance."

Without hesitation, everyone gave Pan their enthusiastic support. They would go to Scotland, to Fiona's castle. With Pan's powers getting stronger, he told Ginger that he would be able to safely transport them through the thin place using the powers from his ring. "This black stone is a teleportation device. Now that I am stronger, I will be able to take us wherever we need to go." Looking at Catriona affectionately, he took her hand.

"There is a necklace that belongs to you. As soon as we free Becky, I will make sure it is returned to you."

Catriona gave him a puzzled look. "How did you know about the necklace? My mother told me when I was a young girl that this special necklace belonged to me. She showed it to me but refused to let me wear it. In my copy of the diary my mother wrote that she had hidden it inside the castle in Scotland, and that she did not want me to wear it."

"I know a lot about that necklace. My memories are returning. I know that the necklace is a celestial navigator. There are two of them. One belongs to you and the other one I hope is not in Beira's hands. Only the rightful owner of the celestial navigator should be able to control it. But if Beira gets one or both of them it will cripple us in our plans to defeat her."

"What's the plan?" Blaze asked. "I for one am ready for battle!"

"The plan will be revealed when we get there and see what we are dealing with," Pan said. "We will remain a safe distance from the house. We'll approach quietly and surprise anyone that might be waiting to ambush us. What do you think, Ginger? What did you see in your vision about Becky? Is Beira there?"

Ginger's gaze turned downward. "I didn't see Beira in my vision. Only Marin, and she had revealed her true allegiance. We will battle her." Ginger hesitated. "And there is another winged creature, black with a red crescent moon under his left eye. I believe we will do battle with him first, and I saw a brief image of him and others, though it was not clear. It faded too fast. I saw Becky and Fiona in a small room that appeared to be in a high tower. They did not see us or know we were there. They appeared to be hiding, and Fiona was holding a glass lock. That was the last image I saw of Scotland. But there is something else. Pan, can you send Rothschild back to the farmhouse?"

"What? Send me back? I want to help. You can trust me. I am *not* with Marin. This is ridiculous! I want to help!"

"I know you aren't with her, Rothschild," Ginger said, "but she is connected to you somehow, and I could feel it in my vision. If you come with us, she will know we are there, and we cannot allow her to be tipped off. Trust me, Rothschild. We will need you when we return, but make sure you stay a safe distance from the house."

Rothschild considered arguing, then with a huff he kicked the ground with his feet. "Okay I will go back. Is there anything else I should do while I wait?"

"Your time will come," Pan encouraged. "This will ensure that we make a surprise entrance. Thank you, Rothschild."

"Remember, stay away from the house," Ginger reminded Rothschild. "Stay hidden, and watch."

Pan held out his arm signaling he was ready to send Rothschild back to Vermont. Rothschild flew over and walked carefully to Pan's hand. The mantis got near the ring and then disappeared.

"Just like magic," Norm chuckled. "Guess it's our turn."

Pan touched his scepter to his ring. Sparks flew from the black stone and a large portal appeared.

CHAPTER 18

Better fifty enemies outside the house than one within.

—IRISH PROVERB

With one magical step, they left The Hidden and appeared on the edge of Fiona's Scottish estate. It was late morning and the sun shone in a cloudless sky. The air was crisp. It was a beautiful autumn day, and there was no indication of trouble. They could see the castle sitting at the center of the estate on a scenic hillside surrounded by meadow, gardens and a large lake. Norm sniffed the air and Ginger followed, lifting her nose. The prevailing winds were blowing from the direction of the castle, and gave them the perfect conditions to sniff out any hidden danger. Norm's nose crystals were muffled, dark, reassuring them that it was safe, at least for now. Blaze huddled close, his breath sending puffs of warm, white smoke into the chilly air. Everyone remained quiet, listening and watching for signs of activity.

"Let's make a move." Blaze whispered. "Send me now. I am ready."

"Patience," Pan replied. "I am not convinced it is safe."

"I can go into the house and remain unseen," Tilly offered.

"Send me." June insisted.

Pan shot a stern glance at them. "I will tell you who goes, and when."

Ginger focused on trying to conjure a vision, but nothing came into her mind. "I'm not seeing anything. No visions, nothing that can help us."

"We don't know what powers you will have here in the mortal world, Ginger. There is a lot we do not know about Sidhe Seers. You are very rare."

Xanderena moved to get closer to Pan. Leaning over to him she whispered, "Marin must be here. She could be inside the castle. What weapons will we use to fight her?"

Pan looked down at his scepter and smiled at her. "We have plenty of firepower. We will know when we should enter the castle."

They waited quietly, trusting Pan's prediction, each watching the castle for signs of movement. The sun was high, indicating that it was noon or even later, when Ginger saw something approaching the castle, flying low over the lake. It was a large, winged creature.

Catriona frowned. "That is not Marin."

They watched as it flew over the castle, hugging the ground, circled, then flew towards them.

"Looking for us?" Blaze asked Pan.

"I don't think so," Pan responded as he looked at the others. "Nobody is glowing. Norm, your nose is still turned off?"

The creature's glide path dipped close enough for them to get a look at red crescent moon markings under its left eye. Ginger shivered, her hair bristling on her back, and wrinkled her nose instinctively, preparing to growl. Pan touched her back signaling for her to stand down. Norm gave Blaze a look, expecting to see smoke billowing, but he remained still, his breathing controlled, eyes focused on the creature, intently studying it as it approached.

"Do you recognize it?" Norm whispered to Blaze.

Blaze's eyes never left the creature, but he frowned, acknowledging that he heard the question.

Then it happened. With an unexpected downward turn, the creature flew close. Norm's nose lit up, blasting a red beacon into the creature's eyes, momentarily blinding it. They watched as it screeched, then careened closer to the ground attempting to flee from the blinding light. Any minute it would regain its eyesight and find them. With the element of surprise gone, Pan held his scepter to the sky, pointing it at the creature, and then took aim and fired, sending out a violent spray of flaming pellets.

The creature angled its wings back and flew skyward. Then two of the flaming projectiles hit, and the creature screamed with pain, its wings flapping wildly as it fell toward the ground. They watched as the dragon then repaired the damage in mid-air, releasing an icy spray over its wings to extinguish the flames.

"It is an ice dragon, but I have never seen one like this before. Never one that looks like this," Blaze whispered. "It shouldn't be able to survive in this warmth."

The dragon glared at Pan as it flew upward.

"I am torching it before it gets away!" Blaze yelled

"I don't think it's trying to get away," Pan yelled.

Ginger's coat stood on end; her eyes glowed as another vision flashed in her mind. Before she could speak, the creature turned and breathed a wall of fire at them, sending them running in all directions for safety.

Blaze took flight. "No more defense. I am going into attack mode." He flew towards the creature.

Pan held up the scepter again, taking aim. "Wait, Blaze, I can take it down," he yelled. "Blaze, I need you to steer clear."

It was too late. The two dragons were locked in battle, flying in large sweeping circles, blowing and spitting fire at each other. Blaze took control by sending powerful bursts of flame at the creature's head and wings. The ice dragon emitted soulful screeches of pain but responded with an assault of razor-sharp ice pellets that it fired at Blaze's head and wings.

Blaze continued his attack on the dragon, setting its wings on fire again and again, but his foe repeatedly extinguished the flames with its icy shield. Blaze flew closer for another attack. As he approached, he blew fiery embers, hoping to force the creature to land.

Frustrated, Pan held his scepter up to take aim. "I am afraid to shoot. I might hit Blaze."

"What is that terrible sound it is making?" Catriona asked as she covered her ears.

"It's calling for help," Tilly answered. "If others come, it will be too much for Blaze."

"You are correct," Xanderena shouted, as she, Tilly and June flew toward the battle.

Just as they approached, the creature blew a giant blast, this time accompanied by fire, onto Blaze's wing. The black plume had a terrible smell of something combustible. The flames engulfed Blaze's left wing and then there sounded an explosion. Blaze flapped helplessly as he tried to stay airborne, but his wing was covered in a thick black tar-like substance. Fighting against the smoldering weight, he screeched in agony as he careened toward the ground. He stopped flapping his uninjured wing and fell into a nosedive. Swiftly they flew to him, creating a shimmery net that wrapped around Blaze as he continued to spiral, unconscious.

The ice dragon was also injured, but before retreating to repair his burning wings, he pummeled them with wet snow and ice as the others struggled to halt Blaze's free fall. Even though they were weighed down by ice, they continued, working together to slow Blaze's descent. Using all their strength, they hovered in mid-air with their friend tucked in their enormous magical pouch. Once they had gained control, they gently lowered Blaze to the ground where June went to work on his burns. She grabbed a handful of meadow grass and yew, rubbing it between her palms until sparks flew from between her fingers. She hovered over his wings, dropping shimmery mixture over the injury. Xanderena joined in until the wounds were completely covered.

Pan watched the injured ice dragon. As soon as it came back into range, he raised his scepter and fired until the creature spiraled to the ground, unconscious.

Blaze struggled to his feet, already feeling the healing effects of the fairy magic. He stretched out his wings and bounded over to the unconscious ice dragon. The others followed him.

"Is it dead?" Norm asked. His nose was glowing an alarm.

"Not yet," Blaze replied, hyperventilating, as he prepared to finish off his enemy.

"Wait!" Pan shouted. "Maybe we can discover something. Who sent him, and how many more are out there?"

"This thing is too dangerous, and as Tilly said it's probably signaled to more of them to come here. We all heard that wailing sound it made. If it wakes up and blasts even one fireball, you are all toast."

Blaze inhaled again, "Let me put an end to him, now."

Ginger stepped up to the creature and placed her paw on it. Her eyes were glowing.

"What is wrong with her?" Catriona called.

"Ginger is having a vision," said Norm.

Ginger's eyes glowed and she stared ahead with a blank expression. Her tail wagged, brushing against the ice dragon. She placed both front paws on it, but it remained unconscious.

When Ginger emerged from the vision, her eyes returned to normal and she walked over to where her friends were waiting. "More like him are coming. A lot more. Marin is outside the castle. Becky and Fiona are hiding from her, in the tower. Something is preventing Marin from reaching them. This creature's name is Crispin, but it is not with Beira. In my vision, I saw it trying to attack Marin and help Becky and Fiona, but Marin had driven it off."

"Why did it attack us?" Blaze huffed. "That makes no sense, Ginger. If this thing isn't with Beira, why is it here?"

Everyone looked at the unconscious dragon, perplexed. Pan asked Ginger, "Are you sure it attacked Marin? Are you sure it means us no harm? Is that what you are saying, Ginger? This thing almost killed Blaze."

Blaze countered, "I was doing just fine. My wing was a little singed but . . . well, I am glad you were there to rescue me."

Xanderena looked at the ice dragon with compassion. "I think we scared him. For all he knew, we were with Marin. I think we should try to speak with him when he wakes."

Catriona wrinkled her nose. "I hate that idea. I think we should leave while it is still—"

Rumbling sounds came from Crispin as he awakened and struggled to get up, and they felt a rush of cold air coming from his nostrils. His eyes fluttered, then opened wide with fear, revealing one eye that was blue-white, the other eye crimson red.

Pan took a careful step toward the dragon with his arm extended and softly spoke. "We did not mean to hurt you. Take it easy."

The dragon's eyes narrowed as he stared blankly at them. His ice-blue eye gave the appearance of friendship, but the red eye sparked anger. After a moment his gaze shifted, moving his eyes carefully at each of them until he found Blaze. His breathing grew faster, sending cold puffs of air blowing towards Norm, who was standing the closest. Norm trotted over to Ginger and stood close to her warm fur. The light from Norm's glowing nose caught the dragon's attention, sending him quickly into a defensive, on-edge posture. A reflexive puff of flames billowed out of his nostrils.

"You really are a unique dragon," said Ginger, who moved closer, unafraid. "You breathe heat and cold." Looking at her friends, she repeated to them, "I don't think he will hurt us."

"Crispin, we are enemies of Beira. Our friend Ginger has seen in a vision that you are an enemy of Marin, and we hope, of Beira as well." Pan reached out his hand in friendship.

"Why did you attack me?" the ice dragon replied, standing tall, searching for Blaze who had shifted to stand behind him.

"It was a mistake," Pan reassured him. "Our friend Norm," pointing to the glowing nose, "has this beacon, as you can see. It glows whenever there is danger, and it flashed into your eyes. Naturally, you attacked and, well, everything happened so fast. Please accept our apology. Blaze, want to introduce yourself to our friend?"

Blaze made no movement.

"Blaze, please, introduce yourself," Ginger insisted.

The stare-down between the two dragons continued until Catriona moved between them, clearing her throat. "There is an ancient diary that has been in my family for a very long time. I have read about you, and your kind. The diary describes powerful dragons that command both fire and ice. You were once friends of my ancestors, the Aos Si."

"You know the Aos Si?" Crispin asked.

"My name is Pan. I am Aos Si," Pan said, "And so are my two sisters, Xanderena and June. This is Tilly, she too is Aos Si. Blaze, Norm and Ginger are with us. You have already met Catriona. Beira cast a spell that—"

Crispin jumped up. "I know who you are. For hundreds of years we have heard rumors about you and how Beira locked you away, rendering you powerless. All the while she has grown very strong, recruiting many of the remaining Aos Si over to her side. Many of the shapeshifters, like Marin, are loyal to her. There are fewer than fifty of us left and we have been fighting her and those loyal to her ever since she tried to stake a claim to our sacred lands. Beira must know that you have been freed. Marin is here. She is inside the outer castle walls, trying to get to the girl and the woman. I came to the castle to see the woman, Fiona, hoping that she would give us an object that we believe can help us defeat Beira. Now that you are free, we can fight Beira together."

"*You* are the dragon that I saw in my vision at the waterfall, before I retrieved the key that freed Pan," said Ginger. "I saw you with the winged girl who took Becky and Fiona."

"That is Olwen. Yes. She fights with us, to defeat Beira." Crispin said.

"You know more than you are telling us," Ginger insisted. She put her paw on the ice dragon. Her eyes started to glow.

CHAPTER 19

Your feet will take you where your heart is.

—IRISH PROVERB

ours earlier, Fiona and Becky had awakened from Olwen's spell without any recollection of what had happened or how they arrived at Fiona's Scottish castle. From the attic tower where Olwen had placed them, they watched from the window as the battle between the two dragons illuminated the late afternoon sky. A gossamer cocoon shielded the door, blocking them from leaving. Every time they approached the barricade tiny sparks flew, warning them to stay away. But it was not that they wanted to leave; in fact, they felt safest right where they were.

Whether it was the remnants of the spell or because of exhaustion, neither of them felt like trying to solve the mystery. Becky had no concern for anyone or anything outside that room. The castle felt like home to her. This was where she was supposed to be. Fiona's former worries about the dollhouse and Catriona had drifted away. She sat with her legs folded up like a pretzel, cheerfully chatting about her early years growing up in the castle. She recalled the visit that Becky's father had made so many years ago, when he was much younger.

Olwen sat on a high wooden beam that hugged the attic ceiling, silently observing their conversation. When Ginger's paw had connected to Crispin, Olwen had felt an electric jolt pulse through her body. She shifted her gaze to the view out the window as she searched the meadow to confirm that her plans had finally come to fruition. When she was satisfied, she drew in a slow deep breath, opening her wings as she dropped to the floor, and landing in the center of the room.

"Everything that has been planned and hoped for is coming to pass. It is time." She approached Becky and touched her on the cheek. "Awaken and see me." Olwen spoke forcefully as she looked into Becky's eyes to ensure that the hypnotic spell would be broken. When she saw recognition in Becky's expression she glided to Fiona and spoke the same command.

As Fiona and Becky oriented to their surroundings, fear gripped them both. Becky felt her knees weaken. "I feel sick." She looked at Olwen helplessly.

Her mind raced as she attempted to retrace the last thing she remembered. She had been at the farmhouse. How did she get back here and who was this winged creature? Did it mean them harm? Where was Ginger?

"Is Ginger here?" she said drowsily. Becky tried to steady herself, but she stumbled. Olwen was there, wrapping her wings around Becky, anticipating that she was about to faint.

"You are fine. I will not let you fall. I have watched you since you were a baby, and I will not let you fall." Olwen's words startled as well as reassured Becky. Olwen's voice was so familiar. All of Becky's worries subsided as she stared into Olwen's eyes, searching for memories of her from childhood. Olwen held Becky, patiently waiting until she was steady on her feet.

Becky saw the necklace that hung around Olwen's neck. She

reached out to touch it. "What kind of necklace is this? It seems familiar to me."

Olwen smiled at Becky as she reached to remove the pendant so that Becky could hold it. "This is a celestial navigator. It is very old and very powerful. Soon you will wear it, as you are the rightful owner."

"I am the owner?" She held the necklace in her hand. *What could a celestial navigator do?* she wondered. Celestial meant stars, and navigate meant finding a path to travel.

"What will I do with this?"

"There is much for you to learn. Too much has been *falaichte.*"

"That word. I have heard it before. *Fallen hatchet.* It sounds like you said fallen hatchet. That is what I heard my teacher say when she was possessed, that day when all this started in my class."

"*Falaichte.* It is a Gaelic word that means *hidden.* It was a warning for you, from me, to prepare you. Our friends will be here soon. Ginger is with them. I have summoned them, and they will arrive. Rest now. You will need your strength. There is much you need to discover about your family, and about yourself, but feel confident that you are not alone." Olwen smiled at Becky and then offered Fiona a brief nod of reassurance. "Fiona, the necklace that you found is the other part of the celestial navigator. My powers have kept it safe from Beira, but she is getting stronger. We cannot let her control the celestial navigators. I know you have many questions. Soon they will be answered."

Fiona looked at the necklace and then back at Olwen. "It was you. You were in the airplane with me that day I came to Vermont. You are the girl. She, you, had the celestial navigator . . . but how?"

"I have watched over your family for a long time, and especially Becky. You see me now, in my true form, but I am able to take the form of a mortal. There was an evil creature following you that day, and I needed to make sure you arrived safely in Vermont."

Fiona felt for her hairpin and realized that it was gone. "The jeweled hairpin that belonged to my mother. I have lost it. She told me to keep it safe. She said it would protect our family, but I have lost it."

"You have not lost it, Fiona. You came to Vermont in search of the key, but all that time the key was in your possession. The hairpin was the key, and you have safeguarded it. Becky placed the key into the stream the same night I placed you both under the spell and brought you here for safety."

CHAPTER 20

There are no strangers here, only friends you haven't met.

—WILLIAM BUTLER YEATS

"Ginger is reading his thoughts," Norm whispered. His nose was glowing, signaling that something was wrong. The tip became crimson, and puffs of steam drifted from his nostrils as his breath mingled with the cool air. With his eyes fixed on Crispin, Norm moved toward the ice dragon to join Ginger.

"This trance is different from the others," Blaze whispered.

Crispin's eyes were locked on Ginger. His flickering blue eye alternated between bright turquoise and a dull icy gray. His red eye glowed a steady warm crimson.

Pan took a step closer and reached out to touch Ginger's fur. "What if he is doing something to hurt them? I don't like this."

Xanderena flew beside Ginger and touched her back while maintaining a commanding gaze into Crispin's eyes. The others gathered in a semi-circle around Norm and Ginger.

Ginger exposed her teeth in a menacing, low growl. Norm was locked into the hypnotic trance. His eyes were glowing, and he hovered above the ground while his feet moved in a swimming motion.

Pan took a step back and silently motioned for the others to follow him. "I think we should wait and give this a little time. I trust Ginger's abilities as a Sidhe Seer. Norm should be fine, too. If anything happens, we will step in and pull them out."

The others agreed, but they all remained on guard.

Tilly stared at the horizon. "Do you think there will be more ice dragons arriving?"

The sun was setting. The castle was falling into twilight. The only light came from one of the rooms in the high tower. Pointing to the castle, Catriona whispered, "That is where we will find Fiona and Becky. We need to get inside the castle. Others will be coming. I feel it. All of us together, we can defeat Marin. With Pan's magic we can get inside."

"Are you ready to do battle with Marin?" Pan probed. "All this time Marin was able to deceive you. Catriona, it is my plan to send you back to The Hidden to wait."

"No, I won't go! I am coming with you. I must see what is inside the castle; and I need to find Fiona and Becky. I will not be turned away." Catriona stared in defiance at Pan.

"We need everyone here. I think she should come," Xanderena joined Catriona, but looked at Pan for his approval.

Before Pan could respond, Blaze blew a burst of hot air in their direction. "Ginger is out of the trance."

The group crowded around Ginger and Norm, anxious to hear what Ginger would say, but it was Crispin who spoke. His eyes had returned to normal, but his expression was alarming.

"I am leaving to get other ice dragons to join in this fight, and I will return as swiftly as possible." Without a backward glance, Crispin extended his wings and soared towards the tree line. Ginger watched him disappear as the sun fell behind the trees and the last traces of indigo and pink faded from the horizon.

Ginger turned to face her friends, her brown eyes still glowing from the trance. She seemed far away as she said, "Olwen has covered the castle with a protective cocoon that only she can penetrate. It is keeping Marin from getting inside."

"Who is Olwen?" Pan asked. "Tell us everything you learned."

With her eyes fixed on the castle, Ginger spoke in slow monotone whispers. Her eyes moved back and forth, as if she was reading from a book. "Olwen is the one who led us here. None of us are in this place by accident. It was Olwen who brought me to Vermont when I was just a puppy, as a guardian over Becky. She brought Fiona and Becky to the tower. Olwen is with them now, in the tower, and they are safe. Soon, Crispin will return with the others."

Ginger turned to face Pan, but her eyes were still glazed from the trance. Norm remained motionless, not speaking or blinking.

"Something is wrong with her," Blaze huffed. "That ice dragon did something to them right under our noses." He shook Ginger. Blowing warm air in her face, he shouted, "Snap out of it."

Ginger stared at him expressionless, her eyes glowing. Tilly, Catriona and Xanderena examined her. "Ginger, are you alright? Tell us our names," Tilly pleaded.

Wagging her tail, Ginger emerged from the vision. "You are so silly. I know who you are. We are fine. Olwen knew we were coming here. She put this information into Crispin's mind because she knows that I am a Sidhe Seer. Now I know what must happen if we are to defeat Beira, rescue Becky, return Pan to power and free—"

Ginger stopped speaking and walked to the edge of the field just as the sun finally disappeared. Pan raised his scepter to cast a magical spell that sent thousands of twinkling glow bugs to illuminate the ground. Blaze exhaled a warm blast of fire into the night sky, and they watched as the embers drifted through the chilly night air, burning out before they reached the ground. The light from the castle tower shone like a welcoming beacon in the darkness. Ginger stared at the castle tower.

"It is time. Olwen is ready for us," Ginger said. "Pan, use your magic and get us inside."

Pan raised the scepter again and the glow bugs swirled around them forming a vortex that stretched skyward. They were transported into the room where Becky, Fiona and Olwen were waiting.

CHAPTER 21

The longest road out is the shortest road home.

—IRISH PROVERB

Becky saw Ginger and bolted past the others while Ginger skidded across the floor in a thunderous *flop, flop, flop* and charged into Becky's lap. At that moment, everyone forgot the challenges ahead and watched the happy reunion. Ginger licked Becky's face as Becky ran her hands down Ginger's long, soft ears. Blaze blinked back dragon tears and sputtered pink smoke as he watched.

"Rothschild should be here to see this," Blaze said. The battle-ready dragon had, at least for the moment, abandoned any desire to wage a war against anyone, anywhere.

Pan stepped away from his friends as they crowded around Becky and Ginger. He barely heard their introductions as each took their turn to meet Becky and Fiona. Their laughter faded into the background as he allowed himself to think back to the day, so long ago, when he had met Olwen. It was just before Beira trapped him and cast her spell on him. He did not want to recall those fateful hours, but he forced himself back. His memories of Olwen were incomplete, but he remembered the fierce determination in her eyes. Those same eyes were staring at him now. He had dismissed her warning when she told him that Beira had set a trap for him and that he was in danger. There was more. What else had she warned him about? The happy sounds of his friends intruded on his memories.

Pan watched his friends as they enjoyed their reunion. Catriona and Fiona were hugging and talking to each other. Their laughter brought a brief smile to his face, and he longed to join them. He wanted to celebrate. He wanted to forget about Marin and Beira, but he did not have that luxury. Pan considered transporting them all back to The Hidden while the celebration was still happening. He did not need anyone's permission. Olwen's involvement meant that time was running out for the mortal world and possibly for all of them.

It was time for him to lead. As such, he took an inventory of his assets—his dragons, Blaze and now Crispin, Norm and whatever powers Ginger possessed, and of course Tilly. Olwen was certainly a big asset and he needed to speak with her, alone, to discuss her role in getting them this far. He had underestimated her once before. He would not repeat that mistake. Catriona, Fiona, and Becky were still a mystery to him, and Olwen had brought Becky here for a reason. Her family appeared to be the focus for Beira's attack.

Pan's decision was made. He raised the scepter to send them all back to The Hidden. As the scepter touched the floor, he heard Becky ask, "Where are my parents?"

The scepter tapped the floor creating the vortex. He raised the scepter toward the ceiling as his surprised friends froze in place. Olwen gave him a smile that encouraged him that this was the correct decision. When the scepter tapped the floor the second time they were transported back to the entrance to The Hidden.

Everyone looked at Pan, perplexed that he had taken matters into his own hands without discussion, but they waited for him to speak. Even Blaze remained silent.

Pan approached Becky. "You asked about your parents. They should be safe for now, but they are frozen inside your house by an evil spell. Do you remember the strange events that were happening back home? I was trapped in the dollhouse that Ginger found and now I have been freed, but there is an evil one that has taken an interest in your family. There is a conflict that started generations ago between your family back in the mortal world, and dark forces here, in this place. There is much for you to learn. I promise, we will return to your home and rescue your parents. We have discovered that Ginger is not just a basset hound. That probably doesn't surprise you. I am convinced that you are not just a mortal girl here by accident. Soon we will take you back home. This time we will be ready for whatever waits for us."

Becky listened to every word as she reflected on the events in Vermont. She remembered the objects hidden in the floor of her room that she had discovered on the night she found Ginger. She thought about New York, back when life seemed normal, and realized that, even then, there had been something that felt wrong. Something counterfeit. For the first time in a long time, she felt calm. The questions she wanted to ask her parents did not seem to matter now because she realized that, whether they had been keeping family secrets from her or not, this is where she was supposed to be, and that all truths would be revealed in their proper time.

"I feel like I have been here before. How is that possible? This place feels like home to me, more than any place I have ever been in my life. From the first night I found you, Ginger, I knew we were connected in a special way. I never gave up the belief that you possess superpowers. I am glad we can talk to each other. Tell me about what happened the night Olwen arrived in Vermont, and about all the things that happened on your journey to find me. Tell me everything."

Ginger walked with Becky past the waterfall that was the entrance into The Hidden, and made their way to the stream. Norm followed and listened as Ginger spoke and Becky understood. There were many things Ginger wanted to share with Becky about the morning Ginger woke to find Becky missing, her parents frozen, and the house blanketed in snow. Ginger was glad that Becky could understand her.

Becky listened as Ginger shared everything that had happened since the night that Olwen had taken her and Fiona. Ginger had transformed from her clumsy puppy self into this graceful, bold, and confident creature. Becky knew that there was much for her to learn about Ginger, the Sidhe Seer.

Olwen and Pan walked together along a rocky and forgotten path towards the overgrown remains of a castle. It was at the castle ruins where Olwen wanted to show Pan something that would be helpful in the battle against Beira. Their voices were quiet as they made their way along the sloping path, and the others watched them disappear deeper into The Hidden.

Before they departed, Pan instructed them to meet back at the waterfall where Ginger, Norm and Becky would be waiting.

"When should we go to the waterfall?" Blaze asked. "Maybe I should go with you."

Pan grinned, "I will send you a signal, one that you will be unable to miss. It will not be hidden from you, my friend."

Hours later, everyone but Olwen and Pan had gathered at the river's edge near the entrance to The Hidden. Norm sat on a large rock partially submerged in the cool water, while Becky and Ginger walked around the water's edge, still talking about Ginger's new powers and especially her sense of smell. Catriona had joined them to discuss their shared family history.

Blaze cautiously watched the sky. "I wonder when or if we will see Crispin and his ice dragon friends?"

"Maybe there are more dragons like you, Blaze. Wouldn't that be nice?" Tilly gave Blaze a playful nudge.

"Wonder what Rothschild found back at the farmhouse? Whatever he found I know he is safely hidden. He is a master at incognito." *Incognito* ended in a gurgle as he put his nose in the water to playfully blow bubbles.

The others laughed, then everyone became silent until Tilly spoke. "We should see something from Pan and Olwen very soon."

Just then a flaming streak of light shot skyward from the castle ruins. Fiona was the first to see it. "There it is! Pan's signal to us." The light was followed by a series of blasts that looked like Roman candles being fired into the sky.

"We have been summoned," said Blaze. "Let's head out."

They made their way along the same rocky path Pan and Olwen had traveled earlier. It was a short walk to the castle ruins. Norm gasped with surprise, "I've been here before. I was teleported to this place, but the castle sat on a cliff with the sea below. There was a girl, and she spoke to me."

"Yes, Norm. You were transported to the castle. Well, a version of this castle. I am going to let Olwen explain what she discovered." Pan stepped back to let Olwen speak.

"This castle is only the remnants of a magical castle that existed a very long time ago in the mortal world. Ancestors of Catriona, Fiona, and Becky lived in the castle and they were guardians of the powerful magic hidden there. Our ancestors trusted that they would use our magic for good. They also ensured that some of our secrets could be kept safe from the evil that exists in the mortal world, as well as in our world. I know this because I found this book which I believed, and still believe, contains the true recording of the events that happened here. Before Beira attacked Pan, I went to him carrying warnings about a plot to kill him. I was not very convincing. I could not get Pan to come with me to read what I had discovered. What is even stranger is that this castle appears here in The Hidden, but then it disappears. I do not know where it goes. Beira is searching for the celestial navigators. Becky is the rightful owner of this one. Catriona, your celestial navigator is safe, back at the castle in Scotland where it is still under my protective spell. Long ago it was your family that guarded our most powerful artifacts. That is why Beira is attacking the farmhouse. She believes some of those items are there. When Pan was inside the dollhouse, it kept her from reaching the items. Now I don't know what keeps Beira away."

Pan touched Becky's shoulder. "The book predicts that there will be another in your family who is destined to oversee and guard the hidden items. This guard will be a girl with a gift to perceive the imperceptible, and the one destined to wear the celestial navigator. That girl is you."

The words sent chills down Becky's back, as she considered what Olwen meant. She felt an adrenaline rush. Unblinking, she stared at the book that Olwen held open, as she let the reality settle over her, and she steadied her breathing.

"Do not be fearful. We are with you now. Everything is happening just as it should. I sent Ginger to you and she will be your powerful ally."

They gathered around Becky, and she felt their strong bond of friendship. "Yes, this is where I belong. I am ready. Tell me what happens next," Becky said.

"Now that Pan is free, we will return to the farmhouse to face Beira. The items that are hidden there will be our weapons. It is the place where your destiny will be revealed," Olwen said, nodding to Pan, signaling that it was time to leave.

"The night that I found Ginger, I discovered hidden items underneath the floor of my bedroom. We must go there first." Becky looked into Ginger's eyes. "There is something in there that belongs to you, Ginger. You were wearing it the night I found you. Pan, will you be able to transport us inside my bedroom? We can get those items before Beira knows we are there."

"Beira is there. At the farmhouse. I can sense her. I see the storm," Ginger said. "The blizzard has covered the house, but the light from the dollhouse still burns. She knows we are coming. Marin is there, searching for Rothschild, but he is safely hidden, down by the pond. We must go. Now."

Ginger's eyes glowed red as her vision faded and her eyes returned to soft brown. "*Go now!*"

"Beira is going to have her hands full." Blaze roared, blowing puffs of smoke as he extended his wings, preparing to take flight.

They gathered into a close circle as Pan raised his scepter. The battle would soon begin.

✦ THE END, BOOK 1 ✦

ACKNOWLEDGMENTS

When our daughter, Kaitlyn, and son, Jordan, were little, they loved for me to tell them stories, but rather than listening to fairytales or something from a Disney movie, they wanted to hear something I made up. Norm, Ginger and the other characters in this book came from those stories.

Years later, my children urged me to write the stories down. I did that, but the longhand versions remained in my desk for a long time—just a stack of handwritten bits and pieces. Again, Kaitlyn and Jordan encouraged me by asking when I planned to do something with my jumble of notes, and I admitted that I could not recall some of the details of the stories. Fortunately, they remembered those stories in great detail. They described the waterfall that guarded the entrance to The Hidden, the glow bugs, and many other details of the stories. That was my motivation to turn the notes into at least one book.

It is one thing to tell stories out loud. Writing them down is much harder! Still, I have enjoyed the process. I am thankful for the encouragement and willingness of my husband, Chip, to read the early drafts and ask the tough questions: that process strengthened the plot and enriched the personalities of the characters.

I want to express my love for my parents, Joe and Betty Jo Hamme. They have always encouraged me to try new things and supported me along the way. Also, my thanks to them for letting me grow up always having at least one dog, and usually more! Animals bring joy to our life and give me inspiration.

I want to thank the readers who have read the work in progress, and those who will read these completed books. I hope it brings joy and inspiration to you!

CPSIA information can be obtained
at www.ICGtesting.com
Printed in the USA
BVHW082253020921
615904BV00004B/841